Hamdi Abu Golayyel, born in Fayoum, Egypt, in 1967, is a writer and a journalist. He is the author of numerous short story collections and novels, including *Thieves in Retirement* and *A Dog with No Tail*, which was awarded the Naguib Mahfouz Medal for Literature in 2008. He is editor-in-chief of the Popular Studies series, which specializes in folklore research, and writes for Arabic news outlets, such as *al-Ittihad* and *al-Safir*.

Humphrey Davies (1947–2021) was a renowned translator of Arabic fiction, historical, and classical texts. A two-time winner of the Saif Ghobash–Banipal Prize for Arabic Literary Translation, he was also the recipient of English PEN's Writers in Translation Award. He translated some twenty works of modern Arabic literature, including Naguib Mahfouz, Elias Khoury, Mourid Barghouti, Alaa Al Aswany, and Bahaa Taher.

T0006946

The Men Who Swallowed the Sun

Hamdi Abu Golayyel

Translated by
Humphrey Davies

hoopoe
AN IMPRINT OF AUC PRESS

First published in 2022 by
Hoopoe
113 Sharia Kasr el Aini, Cairo, Egypt
One Rockefeller Plaza, 10th Floor, New York, NY 10020
www.hoopoefiction.com

Hoopoe is an imprint of The American University in Cairo Press
www.aucpress.com

ISBN 978 1 649 03094 8

Library of Congress Cataloging-in-Publication Data

Names: Abū Julayyil, Ḥamdī, author. | Davies, Humphrey T. (Humphrey
    Taman), translator.
Title: The men who swallowed the sun / Hamdi Abu Golayyel ; translated by
    Humphrey Davies.
Identifiers: LCCN 2021043210 | ISBN 9781649031990 (hardback) | ISBN
    9781649030948 (paperback)
Subjects: LCSH: Bedouins--Egypt--Fiction. | Immigrants--Egypt--Fiction. |
    Emigration and immigration--Fiction. | Marginality, Social--Fiction. |
    LCGFT: Fiction.
Classification: LCC PJ7808.J85 Q5913 2021 | DDC 892.7/37--dc23/eng/20211104

1 2 3 4 5   26 25 24 23 22

Designed by Adam el-Sehemy
Printed in the United States of America

For my friend Suleiman el-Fahd,
the great Kuwaiti writer and historian,
who believed in this novel the most
and urged me to write it.

The Great Leader Himself a Saad-Shin!

USAMA ENDS HIS NOVEL *My Doddery Dog, My Darling Dog* with an appendix. He finished the novel, bethought himself of a new chapter, which he called "a sort of appendix," and stuck it on the end. So I'm going to begin my novel with a fact that may, or may not (I really have no idea), belong here. And that is that the Leader, who invented the Saad-Shin, was a Saad-Shin himself!

Of course, people disagree, as they do with every leader, over the date and place of his birth. One story says he was a Jew, his mother a Jewess from Tel Aviv. Another claims he was of French extraction, his father a pilot who fell from the skies of the Second World War onto the tent of a bunch of Libyan Bedouin roaming around in the desert, and that he married their daughter, who bore him the Leader. Both stories, though, contain ideological elements, justifying the suspicion they were planted by the Leader's historical enemies, the first most likely by the Islamists, who thought he was an infidel, the second by the Leftists, who thought he was a traitor. And talking of the sky from which the Leader's French (supposedly, of course) father fell, it should be noted that the heavens were indeed the Leader's natural element and daily stomping ground: first, because his gaze was fixed upon them and them alone by force of nature, as it were, his neck having an upward curve to it that tilted his face directly toward them (or, as the singer has it, "his head gazing upwards from a desert,

1

ne'er bending but to pray—a horseman who holds horses dear, and camel mares, and sitting grounds where Bedouin of yesteryear hold court"); second, because, when American planes bombed the Leader's house with him inside, he was saved by a miracle that circulated, or was caused to circulate, among our Libyan brothers to the effect that divine intervention had indeed been involved and that a ghostly hand had descended from of the sky to protect him; and third, and most important, because of the Leader's habit of demanding of the highest heavens, in public and in front of everyone, what was he supposed to do with this people of his with whom he had been saddled and against the unbreakable rock of whose appalling, centuries-old pigheadedness all the Leader's theories on good governance, socialism, and equality (as recorded in his *Green Book*) smashed themselves to smithereens? Sometimes he'd forget about the heavens and address the people directly, saying, "Swear to God I don't know what to do with you! You deserve to have the colonists come back and colonize you all over again!"

But forget these two patently planted stories about the Leader's birth. The Leader, my dear friend, was born in the Fayoum, to a family sent running to Egypt, along with so many others, by the Italians, but not, they say, by the Italians as occupiers but by the Italians as fighters defeated in the Second World War, though others say they date back earlier than that and that the family belongs to Egypt's ancient Murabetin tribe of Bedouin. He was born in his maternal uncles' house in the settlement of el-Baraasa in the southern Fayoum, and his mother brought him back as a child to Sirte, from where he moved to Sabha—to the first spark, to the mighty 1st of September Revolution!

Don't think, though, that the reason the Leader invented the Saad-Shin was because he was a Saad-Shin himself. The Leader invented the Saad-Shin because he held such a poor opinion of his own people. They fell short of his ambitions and Third World theories, and he thought that Egypt—Egypt above all—deserved his leadership more. No one believed more than the Leader in the idea of Egypt as Mother of the World. His other thought was that there just weren't enough Libyans. "What's two million on a land area of two million? And if only they were trained! Or educated! Or even just fit for work!"

Anyway, what is sure is that the Leader trusted the Saad-Shin more than the Libyans and chose them for his special operations inside and outside Libya precisely because he had faith in their performance. And it was they who liberated the village of Aouzou and raised over it, for the first time in history, the Libyan flag!

The Wellspring of the Saad-Shin

THE SAAD-SHIN WERE DRAWN from the Bedouin of Egypt or, more accurately, from the Bedouin of all the tribes, including those of Libya. Ethnically speaking, there are two kinds of Bedouin in Egypt—the Bedouin of the east and the Bedouin of the west, and they differ from one another in dialect, dress, traditions, and original homeland. The eastern Bedouin came in waves of emigration from the deserts of the Levant and the northern Arabian peninsula, and share the culture and language of those places. The western Bedouin came in waves from all over the western Sahara, from Morocco to Libya, and share the culture and language of those places.

Geographically speaking, the Bedouin of western Egypt are also of two kinds—the Bedouin of the margins, or of the desert and its borders, and the Bedouin of the sown (or, to be more precise, semi-sown) valley, namely the valley that snakes through the heart of Egypt, through the middle of the desert, from Alexandria to Aswan (note that the inhabited lands of Egypt form no more than three percent of its territory and that the cultivated parts form no more than one percent of its one million square kilometers).

The Bedouin of the margins, whether east or west of the valley, have lain outside the sphere of interest of modern Egypt's central government in Cairo ever since it was founded, following a history of successive occupations of the country, by Muhammad Ali, and they remain so. And not just outside its sphere of interest but a locus of suspicion, wariness, and—these days, in the deserts of Sinai—military conflict. It is a suspicion that, for all its cruelty and the misery it inflicts on these Bedouin of the margins, is not without justification, at least from the perspective of those who harbor it, in part because, among the Bedouin of the margins and the frontiers, in the deserts of Sinai and Matrouh, half the tribe is Egyptian and lives in Egypt, while the other half consists of foreign nationals and lives in a neighboring state. Naturally, things are crueler and have a yet more bitter impact on the life of the Bedouin of the borders when the border in question is shared with a current or former enemy, or one that is crouched waiting to commit aggression during a fragile peace that puts the life of these Bedouin, in all its aspects, on hold. Now, unfortunately, following that "game-changing" Arab Spring, both borders are enemy borders, with Israel, Hamas, and the Islamist terrorist groups on the east and more Islamist terrorist groups on the west, where you can also add Libya's "game-changing" chaos.

Nevertheless, the Bedouin of Matrouh and of the west in general certainly enjoy greater happiness and peace of mind than those of the Sinai desert, who face the ever-present threat of being blown to smithereens. Not to mention that, until a few years ago, the former lived in seclusion, as safe in the isolation of their deserts as it is possible to be, and firm in their belief that Colonel Gaddafi was president of the Arab Republic of Egypt!

More dangerous and more pernicious is the fact that the enemy has moved into Sinai itself and in among its Bedouin. Terrorist Islamist groups have infiltrated and seek to turn it into an Islamic emirate subject to the Islamic caliphate. They are waging a ruinous war with the Egyptian army, with the Bedouin of Sinai caught between the two: if the terrorists set off an explosion, they explode; if the army shells, they're shelled, and all the while both sides, of course, regard them with suspicion. To all of which, add the ancient wounds inflicted on their land and their identity.

About a year ago, the Egyptian government forcibly emptied all the villages of the Sinai Bedouin lying within two kilometers of the border that separates Egypt from Gaza. But that's another issue. Let's stick with the Bedouin of the valley, who originally gave birth to the Saad-Shin. Of course, there were large numbers of Saad-Shin from the deserts of Matrouh and Alexandria, but the Bedouin of the Nile valley were more prone to become Saad-Shin, because half their tribes are actually in Libya and the other half in Egypt.

The Bedouin of the valley, being at its heart, were a matter of concern to the modern state of Egypt since its founding by Muhammad Ali Basha. And how hideous a concern! Security-based, or security pure and simple. You can observe this in the numerous police stations and checkpoints in their neighborhoods. Even for the generation of my father himself, and of his older uncles, the word "government" meant simply the brutal power of the police, who could arrest him for no reason other than that he existed. And this concern certainly had nothing to do with providing any kind of services or utilities. On the contrary, the attitude was like "The best thing would be stop bothering them and leave them as they are." Even after the Bedouin became sedentary and got electricity and other utilities beginning in the seventies, my uncles, when I objected to anything or wrote anything against the government, would say to me in total panic, "But it's the government, Hamdi!"— meaning that brutal power that could send you "behind the sun" where there was no one to restrain them or even witness what happened to you.

Sometimes I think it must be the aftermath of the ancient massacre carried out against their ancestors by Said Basha, who ruled Egypt on behalf of the Ottomans. I had an uncle who pulled every trick he knew until he finally obtained the small government handout known as "Sadat's pension." It was no more than a few pounds a month, but he himself was not at all convinced that he deserved it or that the government had responsibilities of any kind toward him.

As is well known, when Amr ibn el-As "launched his expedition against" (or, to be more straightforward about it, conquered) Egypt at the head of the Islamic Arab army, it was a Roman province, the Romans having occupied it for a hundred years following their expulsion of the Persians. Thus, beginning in 642, Egypt changed from being a possession of the Roman Empire to a possession of the Islamic caliphate, and remained so throughout all its different periods—whatever it was called, wherever its seat might be, and whatever the lineage of its ruling dynasty—until the French expedition against Egypt in 1798. To that point, Egypt had been a subject province ruled by a governor appointed by the caliph, wherever his capital and its location, no matter what he was called or what his title or immortal surname were throughout history—whether he was "Rightly-guided" in Medina or an Umayyad in Damascus or an Abbasid in Baghdad or an Ottoman in Constantinople.

Of course, the Egyptians resisted the French and rose against them in the first and second Cairo uprisings, but until the French expedition they had been barely aware—I might almost go so far as to say had been definitely unaware—of their national identity, or that they were a people or a nation independent of the Islamic caliphate. Following the latter's expulsion in 1801, Egypt reverted automatically, and with the sincere thanksgivings of the Muslim populace, to its status as a possession of the Ottoman caliphate in Turkey.

Which was, by the way, the worst of all the caliphates and occupations, not just in Egypt, but in the whole of history. And I would point out further that Egypt experienced virtually every occupation known to man—Roman, Greek, Byzantine, Arab, Turkish, Persian, Mongolian, and, finally, Western European—and that the Ottoman occupation topped them all, if only because its rule extended for four whole centuries. And all it did during those four centuries by way of assuming the burdens of government was to appoint a governor with an entourage to collect the taxes that he then sent each year, in full, to the Ottoman capital, while the Egyptian people went hungry, was treated to the abuses of enslavement and forced labor, and denied all rights. The Bedouin, on the other hand, under the Ottoman caliphate, took their due, and more, and I believe that the reason for the last of their migrations to Egypt, that of the Rimah tribe, was the affluence that the Bedouin there were enjoying. There they were, on the one hand, free of any control and, on the other, true partners of the Mameluke emirs in the running of the country, each tribe having its encampments and armed militia.

In the same year that the French expedition departed, Muhammad Ali began his rise to power in Egypt—an Ottoman Albanian cavalry soldier married to a rich woman, who bought and sold tobacco and joined the pathetic force that the Ottoman Islamic caliphate had sent to drive the French out of Egypt. And after the British drove them out for them, destroying the French fleet in the Mediterranean, the uprising against Ali Khurshid Basha, the Ottoman caliphate's governor in Egypt, took place, the people rallying round the ambitious Albanian cavalryman, and the notables, merchants, and sheikhs of Egypt choosing him to be its governor, thus creating a rare precedent in the country's history and in that of the Islamic caliphates that had ruled Egypt in succession, for before this, their governor had always been imposed on them from the caliphal capital, wherever that might be. These same people further pressured the Ottoman caliphate until it sent an imperial decree confirming Muhammad Ali Basha as governor. The truth is that the only thing the Ottoman caliphate cared about was the money that came to it from the poll tax imposed on non-Muslims and other taxes, regardless of who, Muhammad Ali or anyone else, ruled Egypt. At the end of the day, though, he was still wasn't a native Egyptian. The main point, however, is that the Egyptians themselves, perhaps under the influence of centuries of enslavement, were not convinced that they were worthy of ruling their own country. True power had always lain in the hands of the Mamelukes and certain armed Bedouin tribes. When Napoleon Bonaparte arrived in Cairo, he assembled its sheikhs, notables, and merchants and asked them to choose provincial governors, that is, local rulers and administrators, from among themselves. They were taken by surprise and asked him contemptuously, "Don't you have any Mamelukes? The common people won't trust us." Muhammad Ali, then, collected the money, in tip-top fashion, for the Ottoman Sublime Porte in his role as master, or (why not say it?) owner, of the lands of Egypt from one end to the other.

Throughout his reign, Muhammad Ali remained an Ottoman governor who owed his governorship, the obedience paid him, and the taxes he collected, to the Ottoman caliph in Constantinople, but at the same time he began to build a modern Egypt on a basis completely independent from the Ottoman caliphate, an Egypt that was an up-to-date sovereign state even if it continued to be, throughout his era, a possession of the Turkish caliphate. Even when he was fighting the Turkish caliphate, and the armies of his son, Ibrahim the Conqueror, were at the gates of its capital, Muhammad Ali was a subject governor who owed his position and his wealth to the Ottoman state.

The main thing is that, in founding modern Egypt, Muhammad Ali encountered two obstacles, each opposed to the establishment of a secure modern state that was stable in terms of its nature, its composition, and its enterprises. The first was the Mameluke emirs, who owned the land as tax farms on which they paid annually what they owed to the Ottoman caliphate but from which they collected many times more than that sum, by using the knout on the peasants. The second was the Bedouin tribes of the west, who lived a nomadic existence, tending their flocks, attacking unresisted the secure, settled villages of the Nile Valley, and joining the Mamelukes in all their wars and raids, in hope of plunder.

The Mamelukes, being, when all's said and done, a minority, were massacred by Muhammad Ali Basha. That's right: he fought them, chased them, and carried out a series of assassinations against them that climaxed in the celebrated slaughter at the Citadel, when he invited all the Mameluke emirs to celebrate his son's wedding, or his own departure for the Pilgrimage, and slit their throats down to the last man at the banquet tables inside the Citadel's walls. For the Bedouin, though—the Bedouin of the west—who were a people and armed and all over the country, in the heart of the Delta and in the Valley, Muhammad Ali prepared a comprehensive political plan based on the carrot and the stick.

Before Muhammad Ali, the western Bedouin had been nomadic—that's to say, real, proper Bedouin—armed and living in tents, which they could set up or fold away at any time and in any place, beyond any control. Among their deeds, the thing they boasted of most, in fact, was their attacks on and their plundering of the villages of the peasants, over and above their on-going fighting for the Mameluke emirs. Muhammad Ali created for them a special protected legal status, termed, in the Egyptian official records, "the Arab Privilege." Special offices and records were established for them with the police and the judiciary, their customary laws and traditions were recognized in cases involving them, and he granted them lands on the margins of the desert, where he let them live in their tents and bear their weapons—on condition that they didn't leave the area of land he had set aside for them. He also excused them from the duty of forced labor and from conscription into the army, a privilege that remained in force until abolished by President Gamal Abd el-Nasser in 1955; the first generation of the Rimah, and of the Bedouin in general, to be conscripted was that born in 1935.

Anyone who rebelled was hung out on Zuweila Gate, in Fatimid Cairo, and many a tribal sheikh was garroted and suspended there for days in punishment for their insubordination and refusal to submit to the authority of Muhammad Ali's state. In the end, his policy succeeded, and generations of Bedouin were born who settled, lived in houses, and worked at tilling the land—something they despised and saw as work unbefitting a Bedouin. Now their villages extend along the fringes of the desert, especially in the northern parts of Upper Egypt.

The last tribe to be forced into submission by Muhammad Ali was the Rimah (plural of *rumh* and meaning "the lances"). They were the remaining core of one of the greatest human migrations in history and they became the core of the Saad-Shin, while at the same time they were a construct of the modern Egyptian state as represented by Muhammad Ali's reforms, just as they were the only Egyptian Bedouin tribe to be proclaimed as such in Egypt and to have no known extensions beyond it. Starting with Muhammad Ali, their sheikh was appointed by the monarch.

Popular narrative derives their ancestry from a young man of the Bani Suleim who fell in love with a girl from the Bani Helal in the encampments in Najd, and when the Bani Helal set off on their celebrated journey to the west, he migrated with them, and they settled in Upper Egypt during the Fatimid period.

The Displacement of the Bani Helal to the West is, of course, well known, in the form of a popular sung (or formerly sung) romance, whose hero is Abu Zeid el-Helali and in which the ancestor of the Rimah is Judge Bedeir. The version told by recorded history, however, favors the theory that the Fatimid caliph el-Mustansir Billah summoned these tribes from Najd in order to increase the numbers of ethnic Arabs on the ground and distributed them around the Delta and Upper Egypt. Because, however, they were fierce and warlike by nature and raiding was for them a form of chivalry and something to

boast of in their odes and verses, they naturally refused to settle down forever in one place among the permanently settled
Egyptian villagers.

At the same time, the uprising by el-Muizz ibn Badis, who
wrested power from the Fatimids and called for a return to
Sunnism, broke out in Tunis, and el-Mustansir's advisers rec-
ommended that he rid himself of these naturally warlike tribes
by sending them off to put down Ibn Badis's uprising. So the
tribes moved westward and put down Ibn Badis's uprising and
roamed around in the Sahara until they reached the Moroccan coast, then returned to Egypt in waves of migration, the
largest of which took place at the end of the seventeenth century. To this day, their villages in the deserts of Egypt remain
almost identical to those in the deserts of Morocco. Scattered
along the fringes of the deserts of el-Minya, Bani Sueif, and
the Fayoum, these are the very villages from which came the
core of the Saad-Shin, who managed to be both Egyptian and
Libyan at the same time.

Gamal Hamdan has it in his book on Libya, its revolution, and its leader-commander, that it was the Bani Suleim
and Helali tribes, with their history of successive waves of
migration, or, to put it more accurately, it was the return of
the Rimah tribe to Egypt at the end of the eighteenth and
beginning of the nineteenth centuries (or earlier, according to
some), that brought the Arabic language to Libya. One thing
is certain, though: before the Muhammad Ali period they
were nomadic Bedouin who never settled in one place.

Their physical features represent every human type.
Some are white as Europeans, others black as Africans. Most
are tall, brown-skinned, handsome, and good talkers, lovers
of speech and poetry. They supported themselves from pas-
toralism, lived in tents, and were always on the move. At the
same time, they were an armed force capable of repelling the
government itself, especially as it wasn't a real government,
just an Ottoman garrison, easily repulsed and defeated.

During the period when Muhammad Ali was at war with the Mamelukes, the Rimah would move their tents and animals into the desert around Beheira; some say that it was only our family that used to move into the Beheira desert and that the other members of the Rimah's forty families were already living, and settled, in northern Upper Egypt. It is also claimed that the movement of the Rimah to northern Upper Egypt, where they took the Fayoum as their center, is attributable to Muhammad Ali's plan to split up the Bedouin—not literally, but to break up their main concentration and mix it into the larger society: a tribe in Beheira was to migrate to the Fayoum and a tribe in the Fayoum to migrate to Beheira and so on.

The fact is, I do not know precisely when the Rimah began their move to northern Upper Egypt. What I do know is that the founder of my family, my great-great-great-great-grandfather, migrated to our present location on the fringes of the desert south of the Fayoum during Muhammad Ali's war with the Mamelukes but that the reason for his migration was something entirely different: it was a court of Bedouin elders that ruled he should "move to new pastures," that is, permanently migrate from where he had been, and the census carried out by the Egyptian government in 1845 has him down as a Bedouin sheikh of eighty years with nine sons, the youngest of whom was one year old, living a settled life in his "enclosure," meaning his house, in the hamlet that to this day bears the name of his son, Saqr Bu Golayyel, in the southernmost part of the Fayoum.

Many of the Saad-Shin are from the Fayoum, and from the Rimah of the Fayoum specifically, and many of them are my neighbors and relatives. The Saad-Shin also included Bedouin from all over Egypt, from el-Minya and from Bani Sueif, but the Fayoum was their hub. The Leader did to them again what the Fatimid el-Mustansir had done to their ancestors but in more "revolutionary" fashion. All the Saad-Shin who were originally from the Fayoum have returned to Egypt and continued with their lives in the Fayoum, but they have never lost their links to Libya and have never stopped being Saad-Shin.

The Saad-Shin

THE SAAD-SHIN, OR SONS of the Eastern Desert, was a nationality invented by the Leader and Commander. For real. This isn't
fiction. That, *The Green Book*, and the Great Manmade River
were all things he thought up by himself. Indeed, it was the only
one of those ideas that was implemented and completed. The
Great Manmade River has still never run, or never run in a
fashion to match its Greatness. The sayings in *The Green Book*
broke, one after another, on the mighty rock of the Libyan people's disdain, the same disdain that, in the end, brought down
the Leader himself. The Saad-Shin, though, gave birth to a lineage, a line, a breed of people, half Egyptian, half Libyan.

The great novelist Llosa wrote his novel *The Feast of the Goat*
about a Latin American dictator who, for all his weirdness and
for all Llosa's exaggerated aggrandizement and disparagement
of him and his legend, was nothing compared to the non-fiction
character of the Leader, whether in his life in general or in his
hideous death. The Leader laid his plans to become a leader
as a fourteen-year-old boy, and he became a leader in reality,
and of a vast country, at twenty. The plan was agreed upon
between him and his classmates at the Sabha middle school,
and in accordance with that plan they entered, first, military
high school, and then the army, and pulled off the famous
coup against King Idris el-Senousi. The Leader then led the
Great Libyan Arab State of the Masses for forty-two years and
the number of traps, dirty tricks, plots, and coup attempts he

survived during that period made his claim to be a prophet seem incontestable. And some of his people did in fact believe in him. Even some foreigners believed in him. An Italian lady of sound mind published a book called *The Leader, Prophet of the Desert* in which she affirmed her belief that the Leader was a prophet upon whom divine inspiration had descended as it had upon other prophets of the desert throughout history. Not to mention his hordes of devotees in other Arab countries. And given that prophets usually end up getting killed, he, in the end, got killed, just like any other prophet killed by his own people.

Leaving aside that our own Prophet, the Prophet of Islam, specifically was *not* killed by his people, the fact that the Mighty Revolution of the 1st of September succeeded so easily proved to the ambitious young revolutionary Leader that he was ruling a land without a people. A land of vast, unguarded wealth, whose greatest paradox was the disparity between its surface area and the number of its inhabitants. He therefore gave nationality to whomever of the young Egyptian Bedouin population he wanted, and these travelled to the Libya of oil in the seventies to work on the basis that they were in origin the offspring of ancient waves of migration from Libya's west. And he would have kept going if the fierce quarrel that broke out between him and Egypt's Leader hadn't put a stop to the project. When it did so, the Leader first added them, along with the other members of the Saad-Shin, to the Libyan army, then collected them into a battalion or, according to some, an entire army that was responsible only to him.

The fact is that the Leader believed in Egypt. He saw it as the strongest of guardians, an unshakeable bastion, and its people as a people worthy of his leadership. Some say too that the initial reason for the granting of nationality to the Saad-Shin went back to his search for someone to lean on in Egypt; not a fifth column, but a strong, resounding voice to defend Libya should it ever be attacked by its enemies, one to defend that unguarded land. Fortunately, this voice existed, was accepted as valid, and was ready to do so—Libya's cousins among the Bedouin of Egypt, who had for so long helped their relatives among the Bedouin of Libya during the Italian occupation. Men such as Hamad Basha el-Basel, who helped Umar el-Mukhtar with money and weapons, and even with his own skillful, brave cavalrymen, and who, when el-Mukhtar died a martyr, held a large memorial ceremony for him in Cairo to which he invited the political, artistic, and even sporting elite, and who, when the authorities banned the banquet in deference to the Italian occupiers, distributed it to the people.

Unfortunately, though, the Leader took the shoddy goods. He gave Libyan nationality to the least educated and competent Bedouin youth, the grindingly impoverished at every level, and that was the main reason for their tragic experience with him and the Leader's with them.

Anyway, the plan was for the Leader to support the young tribesmen of Egypt, granting them Libyan citizenship and providing them with money, opportunities, and privileges, until they attained a position that would allow them to defend Libya if things went bad. Implementation in Egypt began but the Egyptian authorities were irritated that this one specific group of Egyptians should be showered with the Leader's largesse, so implementation was transferred to Libya, and in the seventies he began seducing young men, and especially young Egyptian Bedouin men, into traveling to Libya, where they were given Libyan nationality, jobs, and boundless opportunity. Or perhaps the young men themselves were driven by the force of their poverty and of their hard-scrabble existence in Egypt. And as soon as a young man, or an old one, or anybody of any description, from a Bedouin tribe in Egypt arrived in Libya he would be "identified," meaning taken before an aged Libyan sheikh who would ask him some questions from whose answers the sheikh would deduce the name of his family and his clan in Egypt, and he'd obtain Libyan nationality, on condition that he keep his Egyptian nationality and on the understanding that he would work in Libya, where all fields would be opened to him, and from which he would return to Egypt with enough wealth to assume the role allotted to him in the Leader's plan. The Leader dedicated an official government office, the Desert Bureau, to this operation. It is said to have been gutted by fire following the killing of the Leader, leaving the Saad-Shins with nothing to show they were Saad-Shins or prove that they were Libyan nationals with full rights.

Needless to say, vast masses of Bedouin youth from the Fayoum, el-Minya, Bani Sueif, Matrouh, and Alexandria went, but because they had basically gone in search of work, and because the Egyptians who go abroad fall into three categories, and because these were from the third category, that of the ordinary workers and day-laborers, they had to wait in line—most of them, that is. So they stood in line. They didn't go straight into money-making activities, then make a speedy return to Egypt. Most of them couldn't find work and got little for the work they did do. In brief, they were a burden on the Leader's shoulders, so he decided to make the best of it. He favored them for his special missions. The ones of good background, who were assuredly few, he took for his personal guard and used as his personal bludgeon whenever it entered his mind to bludgeon, and the rest he put into the army, but not just into the army. He sent them off to form a special brigade or regiment, the best of whom he dispatched to a military training course in Italy to learn street fighting. It was these he used to carry out the revolutionary operations that he mounted around the world and with whom he supplied the various far-flung revolutionary associations and organizations of which he was patron. He sent them to help the revolutionaries and rebels of the Philippines, Ireland, Indonesia, and Latin America. It was with them that he liberated the village of Aouzou from Chadian forces, backed by the French army on its mission to patrol the borders of Africa.

The Vermin of Africa

I TRAVELED FOR THE SAME dream, to make the same gearshift
(which wasn't in the end really so much a dream or shift as
a hideous mistake or shambles) just to scrape together a few
pounds to get married so they wouldn't say, "Bu Hamid's boy
couldn't afford to get married, the old buzzard couldn't raise
her own children." *"Buzzard's about right!"*—the last bit of the
sentence, or charge, being added by my paternal uncle, *with
emphasis*. And even though my uncle had his own old buzzard
on his back, his words were like a sword blade to my mother,
who was the only person I have ever seen wince, shudder,
ache, and moan at what he said, and not just at what he said
but also at what my other paternal uncles or paternal aunts or
maternal uncles or maternal aunts or anyone else said. A word
would lift her to the highest heavens, another cast her into the
bowels of the earth, and at the descent of that blade, we fell
to pieces fell to pieces fell to piyiyiyeeeces—which I have to
sing, I swear to God, because we really did fall to pieces fall to
piyiyiyeeeeeeeeeces. There wasn't a man or a woman among
her relations who hadn't poked her in the eye, or whom she
hadn't poked in the eye, with a word. But that's another story.

And I was a good boy. Anyplace you chucked me, I stuck,
and what was going to Libya if not getting chucked? Though
that's another story too.

What matters is that the Phantom Raider made that same
gearshift but by going to Europe, where the gears really shift,

while I decided to do it by going to Sabha, which was one of those decisions that cost me my future. I don't know whether it was a decision, inborn stupidity, or just a unique imbecility.

In the nineties, I'd just come out of the army. It was the year Yasser Arafat's plane crashed in the desert near Sabha. I was close by, in Sabha itself. The brotherly Libyan Army was flailing around lost in the southern desert and had failed completely for two whole days to locate Arafat and his plane. Then some Mediterranean asset of the American navy pointed them out. All the same, when the Leader visited Arafat after he'd been found and taken to the hospital in Sabha, he said, "They're saying the Americans led us to you in the desert! It was our courageous army that got you back!"

"You're not living up to your potential," my mother used to tell me.

I'd answer angrily, "If I lived up to my full potential, I'd be asleep. I'd probably be sleeping like a log. I wouldn't even be moving!"

She'd reply, with annoyance and covert disdain, "Why? You're from the Bu Jalil family and everyone knows it!!" followed by a double exclamation mark for good measure and of course I couldn't tell her that the outer limit of her beloved Bu Jalil family's world was the bridge at the entrance to the village. Sometimes I'd say it was all because of my father. He'd been a government night watchman, which was normal among Bedouin, with most of our relatives being watchmen to begin with, and with all the village heads, without exception, putting their older sons to work as watchmen. My late lamented father, though, used to make out like he was an air pilot or something and was ashamed of it all, poor dear. On occasions when he couldn't get out of having it with him or had to have it inspected by some official, he'd be so embarrassed at carrying a night watchman's rifle he'd hire someone else to carry it for him. Despite which he never left the job. He joined when he was going on fifty and gave up. All he ever wanted to do was sit in a dark room, which I decided must be the grave or something, but I have a friend who whenever I tell him this story says it was depression—"Your father suffered from depression!"— and laughs, I have no idea why, so in the end I got sick of the whole thing.

I'd studied, of course, for about sixteen years, but I hadn't learned anything. I'd taken over the farming from my mother and even though it was the only thing I did well and liked I was a failure at that too, and a resounding failure to boot, unfortunately, which is a story in its own right that I ought to call *The Imbecilities of Agriculture on Thin Soil*—"bad soil," as the peasant who sold me the palm trees that I planted there had said, with the utmost contempt. First off, it was very salty, and when you removed the salt, you found huge rocks, stuck fast and stretching all the way to the end of the holding. But, with my unique stupidity, I insisted on farming it. Enough with the excuses! The truth is, the problem wasn't my studies or my education or even whether I gave things a proper go or not: the problem was my reckless enthusiasm and the way I threw myself into subjects and projects and tasks that I'd never even heard of a moment before.

Though sometimes I feel that failure—in the absolute and quite apart from my personal train-wreck—goes back in the end to options: options for nothing, options for failure; what my first teacher, Mustagab, used to call "the mark of poverty," the same thing that made him, personally, wallow in the pleasures of "red stew." You know red stew? It's the pota-toes-in-tomato-sauce that was all most of our mighty people could hope for. It's the red mark of poverty that makes one slog around blindly in the mud. I mean it, I swear! In the mud! Though what is life anyway if not slogging around in mud?
He'd give anything for the big prize but reaches only for the small. He'd give anything for a front-row seat but makes his way to the back. The easy thing, the thing that's absolutely guaranteed to be within his grasp without his being teased

or having to compete or even with anyone else having to be there. At school, the kids would quarrel over who got to sit at the first desk while he'd keep going, shame-faced and a little anxious, to the back row. In Cairo, for example, the easy thing to do was work selling clothes in el-Ataba.

There were opportunities in journalism, even, but he refused to consider being anything but a construction laborer. Is it the incontestable way-things-are, or is it stupidity, or is it brute force?

I spent a year in Sabha. The extreme southwest, the revolutionary capital of the revolutionary Leader and his even more revolutionary regime; where he'd lived and studied and where the first spark of the 1st of September Revolution, which delivered Libya into his hands for the next forty-two years, was struck. Here he'd founded the first General People's Congress, at which he proclaimed his Third International Theory for the liberation of humankind. He'd tried to make it into a European city, with a variety of extensive gardens, but the people of Sabha—the original inhabitants, the Toubou and Tuareg—understood, or found it convenient to understand, that the gardens were just government pastures with fences round them and parceled them out among the flocks of sheep and goats and herds of camels, and when the authorities made a fuss about their livestock, they parceled the gardens out for fodder, each cropping a particular area. On my rare days off in Sabha, I'd accompany my friend Muhammad el-Targi as he cut fodder for his flocks in the late afternoon in the garden of the General Directorate for Culture and the Arts/Sabha.

Which reminds me (and I'm not even going to try justifying bringing this up): the original Tuareg and Toubou inhabitants of Sabha are the subjects of most of the novels of the celebrated Libyan writer Ibrahim el-Koni who, however, perhaps because of the long time he's lived abroad, has failed to see their reality, or even their history—just their legend, hovering in the skies of el-Ablaq, the Pied Camel; he has failed to see their camels wandering through the garden of the Palace of Culture—just that pied one of theirs, which was so excessively legendary that he could just about gaze into the heavens and commune with them.

Authority in Sabha lay in the hands of the Leader's relations. Forget the government, the Council of Ministers, the officials, even the army and police, most of whom were mercenaries anyway, authority on the street lay with the Leader's relations. It was enough for someone to be a relative of his for all doors to open and all barriers to be broken, in Sabha and in Libya generally. And his relations were of different standings, depending on how closely related to him they were. The absolute bottom rung were the ones who'd returned from other countries, such as Tunisia, Chad, and Niger, and the lowest of these were the ones who'd returned from Egypt, and they were the ones who ran Sabha.

Before the 1ˢᵗ of September Revolution, they were in the middle, tribally speaking, and in Egypt there were plenty of them even though they had "nothing but the shirts on their backs." In our area of Danyal, district of Etsa, the Fayoum, there were three or four families from the Leader's tribe, some of whom were well-off and influential at the national level, like Hajj Ghubashi, who was said to be the Leader's cousin, or even his paternal uncle directly. He was formidable—a tall black man who owned flocks and herds and a plot of land on which he'd built a mosque that he named after himself. The likelihood that he really was related to the Leader was increased by the fact, even at the height of the armed clashes in the seventies between Libya's Leader and Egypt's, his five children could go to and fro between Egypt and Libya, and all of them got the Saad-Shin card, followed by Libyan nationality.

In Sabha, the Leader's relations had once been under the patronage of the Seif el-Nasr family, Sabha's ancient rulers and masters, as well as being part of their inner circle and beneficiaries of their largesse (and the Leader knew the meaning of largesse, witness his later taking charge of his relatives' education and rescuing them from the fate of ending up as poor shepherds in the deserts of Sirte such as he himself had been, or had been on the road to becoming). After the revolution, everything was turned upside down. It was then that the Leader's relations—all of them, pure-bred and half-bred—pounced on the town, which they considered theirs, "something just for them," the pure-breeds becoming its rulers, the half-breeds its thieves. They confiscated everything belonging to their Seif el-Din masters, imprisoned them, then exiled them to Egypt along with their entire families.

When I arrived there, Sabha was in turmoil, on edge, pullulating with people—its original inhabitants, Tuareg and Africans from the northern and southern Sahara, as well as Africans from the rest of the continent. But control was in the hands of the Arabs. Not any Arabs, just the Leader's tribe. The Leader's tribe ruled the whole of Libya, and Sabha was their house and their home territory.

Sabha is the first stop on the route taken by young Africans fleeing toward the European dream. They arrive on foot from the deserts of Niger and the forests of Ghana, always an easy, though sometimes fierce and murderous, prey to Sabha's bullies, its nothing-to-lose youth, and the relatives of the Leader, or the ones who'd made it, most of whom, in Sabha, were police or army officers. Many of its young people were criminals, or if not exactly criminals, thugs, or if not thugs, neighborhood bullies who stole and mugged people, especially Africans and Egyptians, right in front of the police, who were mostly Africans and feared and obeyed them. ("What are you whining about, you pissy little Egyptian? I'm a blood-spattering Gaddafi!")

Sad to say, Egyptians were the ones in Sabha who most often got mugged, more so even than Africans. The mugger, or thug, in Sabha and throughout Libya, is very wary when it comes to Sudanese and Tunisians and is terrified of Algerians but he can't get enough of Egyptians. In the patriotic debates I got into with Eweidat and the Moroccans, I'd always say, "It's what being civilized is all about! Fear is proof of civilization! The difference between the human who's been civilized since ancient times, the primitive Bedouin, and the savage just down from the trees is fear. When a man from the city goes visiting in the forests and swamps, he has to be afraid, terrified, of the savages," and I'd look them in the eye for a moment to show them that if the cap fit . . . But it's a phenomenon, unfortunately, and not just in Sabha but in all the Arab countries. Sabha's just the bottom of the bucket. Egyptians are like that all over the Arab world. Forget the crap about the Egyptian elite with its culture and its history and its "teachers who educated the peoples of the Arab world." It's those same Arab peoples I'm talking about.

Sabha pullulated with the vermin of nations, pullulated with the vermin of Africa—Arab Africa and African Africa and mixed-up Africa. The peoples from the bottom of the heap were there, right there at the bottom of the heap. Even the rulers were from the bottom of the heap, relations of the Leader and Commander but not part of the stable elite that surrounded him in Sirte, most of them little no-account Bedouin from Egypt, Tunisia, Chad, and Niger and making themselves out to be Libyans—the quintessence of the people the Leader himself manufactured, for himself and as his personal property.

Applying my philosophy of always taking the seat at the back of the class, I crossed the whole of Libya and came to a stop in Sabha. Then I left the rest of Sabha behind and settled down among its most dangerous criminals—Bu el-Helb, who'd been condemned to death in Egypt, Jerjaresh, who was on the run from the Uganda operation, Kheweitar, who'd kidnapped the wife of the Yugoslavian doctor, and Bu Abdallah (and only God knows what Bu Abdallah had done). All these winners were my friends and colleagues, who ate and worked with me. I was the innocent naive soul in the middle of a gang of criminals, praying the five daily prayers at the proper times in the heart of Bu Abdallah's brothel and likely to come to a bad end at any moment, but not, until I got back to Egypt, giving a thought as to how dangerous they were or to the risks of living with them.

Jerjaresh had been in a brigade or a company that the Leader sent to help his friend the Ugandan leader, Idi Amin, against the rebels there. While Jerjaresh and his colleagues were circling in the airplane over the outskirts of Kampala, the news arrived that the rebels had overthrown Idi Amin and he'd fled the country. The plane was forced to land at Khartoum airport, which, by a minor miracle, it did, and that was the day he announced that he was *jerjaresh*, meaning, in the Libyan dialect, a wacko, or someone who's been discharged from an insane asylum, and from that day on he became known as Jerjaresh.

This, I'm sorry to say, is a deep-seated trait in me: I'm always the naive soul in the pack of rogues, never noticing what's about to shaft me till it's all the way in. Sometimes I console myself with the thought of the novelist who, like my friend the poet el-Denasuri said, has to be a wood-gatherer, palm-climber, and man-tracker, and suck it all up, but I, personally, am slow to get it. I confess this about myself, so I can grant myself absolution from the whole mess from the start. But what's worse than the slowmindedness is the good intentions. And, as I said, I never know I've been shafted till I've taken it all the way up.

Sabha is the home territory of the Saad-Shin. It's the only place in Libya where they can move around on the basis that they're Libyan citizens, even if there's always the odd sharp-tongued Libyan sheikh to remind them of their origins ("Who does he think he is? Some pissy little Saad-Shin making himself out to be Libyan. Gimme a break!")

I got out of Sabha completely and went to live among the Saad-Shin and their criminals in Tayyouri, the industrial quarter, south of the city on the way to the airport, and I shared in everything they did.

The industrial quarter consisted of rectangular workshops arranged in orderly rows inside low buildings facing onto streets that reminded me, I don't know why, of straight little irrigation ditches, or like they were trying, under the world's hottest sun, to be little irrigation ditches, running through rectangular agricultural plots, and which were always teeming with strapping African youths fleeing toward the dream of Europe.

The Saad-Shin guys had an apartment in a building in Tayyouri, all of them men who'd "returned" from Egypt and joined the Libyan army, from which they were now either retired or on the lam, or were even still on active duty with. Tayyouri was like them—very poor, half shanty town, half government-built, a housing project that had never been finished, which was normal in Libya, a.k.a. the Great State of the Masses (I personally had a Libyan friend who'd gotten a high school certificate in humanities, gone into medicine, and when he failed at medicine, gone into engineering!) built around a dozen residential blocks opening onto a large open space.

In the beginning, Tayyouri Quarter consisted of government-built housing blocks, finished and unfinished. Then it was houses of brick and cement. Then it ended up huts full of Africans.

The Saad-Shin who were my friends lived in the apartment blocks—around forty of them, though usually there wouldn't be more than ten together at one time in an apartment, the rest working or doing whatever or on the run from whatever, and all of them, with the exception of Anwar el-Rumhi and maybe Ba Nour el-Rumhi, were in their forties, men who'd come to Libya in the seventies to work and go back to their families in Egypt but who'd stayed, all of them waiting for the moment when they could return to Egypt and cooking *mebakbaka*—macaroni with meat—in a big cauldron, and all miserable, unwilling to go home as losers with such wasted lives and unable to continue as mercenaries in the Leader's brigades.

The True Definition of the Seid in the Land-of-the-Ear-That-Peeps-From-Under-the-Outfit

THE WORD SEID IN THE Arabic of the western Bedouin doesn't mean, as elsewhere, "the act of hunting" or "the prey" itself. It means the leopard-like lad who's quick and limber, snatches birds from the air, and escapes the clutches of every living thing, or is like the cunning fox that snatches chickens from houses.

And the Seid, the Phantom Raider, was like that—a bird-snatching leopard, tall, dark-skinned, limber and trim-figured, with fiercely focused face and features, and eyes that were frank and trusting even when he was lying. He belonged to the sixth generation, the generation that was supposed to call me "uncle" though he didn't because the age difference was so small. I don't know how to describe my own generation, the fifth. Sometimes I call it the Gas Guzzler Generation; you can call it the Blowhard Generation if you want to be rude. And the generation of the Raider's father—or, to be more accurate, his grandfather, the beloved generation of the sixties—I call the Destitute Generation, or you can call them, if you want to be really rude, the Dismal Failure Generation. Between them was the generation of the seventies. That was the Artists' Generation—everyone striking some kind of pose, writing poetry or painting or writing novels or hanging pictures of naked dancers in the middle of the family reception room, though the strangest thing about them was, I swear (and this was of course a genuine tragedy), that even their features resembled those of the leading lights of the seventies generation of poets in Cairo. I call them the Generation of Bare Heads and Shaven Faces; you can call them the Generation of Certain Doom, if you want to be rude.

Truly, an amazing generation. The least of it is that all of them died early, not one of them, or of those who were well-known, making it to sixty, and every one of them messed up somehow or other, from the headman's son to the night watchman's son, from the member of parliament to the peasant in the field. The strangest thing was that the ones who weren't messed up were the dumbos, the failures and lightweights, the ones who "eat, drink, go to the fields, come back, and fall asleep like dumb animals." And all of them without exception, in each clan branch, hamlet, and family, chose headmen for themselves and from among themselves.

Let me tell you about the hamlets. I mentioned them in *A Dog with No Tail*—the nine hamlets, the nine Bedouin settlements that turned into hamlets, numbered on the map, with schools, police stations, and big soccer clubs that competed in the local league. Every village headman had his life set up just right, had got his children married off, and was exercising his seigneurial rights over every woman within reach. His hamlet was the center of the universe and mother to every other settlement, and you'd better believe it or else! Egypt was the Mother of the Patient and his hamlet was the Mother of the Settlements or, to put it differently, the biggest, hence the refuge and protectress of the rest. So each headman naturally had applied officially to the police station for the headmanship of the lot in accordance with his unshakeable conviction that he was the worthiest and most deserving of them all: "Who dey tink dey are?!" (or "Who do they think they are?" to put it in a way more appropriate to their new-style *galabiya*s and dialect, and their now unturbaned heads).

Our own turn at the headmanship had been delayed—put on hold, officially, for a quarter of a century. You could even say it was completely done for, as a position and in terms of our status and role in society, but we had about six headmen of our own, each of whom played the role at home by opening their reception rooms to everyone, ruling on everyone else's problems, and running to the police every time someone was arrested. And also, of course, by insisting on taking first place in everything and in their greed for the Big Prize.

These were the first of our kind, of our Rimah tribe specifically, to go bareheaded and wear peasant *galabiya*s or, more accurately, the *galabiya*s worn by peasants who had pretensions to being city folk— *galabiya*s with a collar, and a pocket sewn onto the front, at home and in the fields (in photos, a three-piece suit), a change that came about I know not how and just seemed to sweep the board. All of a sudden, they'd taken off their Bedouin *galabiya*s, with the wide sleeves, the striped satin waistcoat and the caftan, and turned into city folk, with bare heads. And with this came amazing changes in the clothes worn by the women in our settlements—liberation, elegance, and a desire for joy and seductiveness, along with the sudden appearance of dresses that were form-fitting, low-cleavaged, and sculpted down to the knees.

In truth, our girls—or let's say some of our girls, or let's say at least a very small number of our more elegantly dressed girls, the ones who loved beauty and clothes and the body and chic, and especially those of the seventies generation—were a wonder to behold when it came to this stuff. Wherever you looked, at the canal or the fields or even the roofs, you'd see glittering colors, *galabiya*s with short sleeves sculpted, I swear to God, to make you laugh and cry, and doing no harm to anyone; on the contrary, all joy and pleasure and pure delight.

The amazing thing, my friend, is that it was the seventies girls the Salafists put back into Modest Dress. I'm talking about the first generation in the unbroken Modest Dress chain that leads all the way to our own day. Of course, the full-face veil launched its assault in the nineties, when our hamlets began turning into black forests of veiled women. The nineties! Ah, the nineties! Light and dark, glad tidings and black clouds, the bitter harvest of el-Sadat and his debauchery. Not just el-Sadat, to be honest: el-Sadat simply took the cover off the poisoned sewer, which then killed him.

Whatever. Let's stick with the seventies. Lots of our girls were very smartly dressed and wore the latest fashions even when veiling was at its height, so there always had to be a little something sticking out, whether it was the ear of a beautiful girl walking with bouncing hair through the middle of that pitch-black forest of veils, or an "ear" of something smart she was wearing. You'd see a girl wearing an outfit in the latest style, with an "ear" of something peeping out from underneath—an "ear" of her pinafore or of her baking *galabiya*, or even her own actual ear, grubby as it might be. I have an aunt called Umayma, very dignified and, to be honest, fierce. She was in charge of making the clothes for the girls of the settlement—its one and only all-powerful seamstress. At weddings and on other social occasions, she'd go around in a green suit topped by a colored peasant head rag with a tall, four-tipped bow.

The Phantom Raider's father was of the same generation (not of my aunt, of the seventies). He was the first to take off his turban, his skullcap, his Bedouin *galabiya*, his caftan, and even his identity as a Bedouin, and walk around on the basis that he was a civilized man of the city. It was of him that the poet said, "Musa, who makes out like he's an effendi and turns me on a Polish radio—what luck, if you want to hear the news!" Back then, there were only two radios in our village and the whole surrounding area, and they were fixed, immovable, and ran on batteries. When TV arrived, the only set was at my uncle Hamza's house, and my uncle Hamza's house had no wall around it. He wasn't rich, he was a night watchman, like my father, but he didn't have a problem with it, even though it was below his station (son of the headman and working as a watchman!). He was also the back-up imam at the mosque if the full-time imam, my uncle, the headman, Abd el-Hamid, was away. His house was spacious and welcoming, and we'd spend our time there—the whole village—till it went off air. The truth is, there aren't any rich people in our village, meaning anyone from the affluent, isolated, rich elite. We all live more or less the same. Anyone who's managed to scrape together a little land has done so basically by living in absolute poverty: "Terrified by poverty and living it," as my maternal uncle Mukhtar used to say. And the generation of my father, my mother, my paternal uncle Hamza, my paternal uncle the headman, and my maternal uncle Mukhtar experienced poverty such as I'm pretty sure no other humans on the face of this earth ever have. They had three months in the year they called "the hunger months" and there was nothing any man or woman among them took greater pride in than saying, "Praise God, we weren't hungry at all!" Once I went back home to my mother in the village while I was on a diet and she said to me, "What's this *die-it*?" so I told her, "You eat a little less."

"Why would you little down your food?" she said. "We couldn't believe our eyes if we found any!"

My paternal uncle Musa, on the other hand, had been rich and pampered from the day he was born and looked like a real prince—white, slender, and clean, with large eyes, a strange spicy smell, and smooth hair that hung down his back. At the height of the days of the battery-powered Polish radio that never left its place (the one of which the poet sang), and at the very time that people were going barefoot and knew nothing of the world beyond the bridge at the entrance to the village, my uncle Musa was taking summer vacations in Alexandria's finest hotels.

Some people think—or, to be precise, my mother thinks—that what spoiled him, or made him so citified that he ended up spoiled, or that held him back and made his days on earth a trial to him, was his overdoing the self-indulgence: "Just like your dad but your dad was different, his mum was a simple soul. Musa, though, was born to a tough old woman, successful and rich." All her men, every one of them, my mother goes on, with some exaggeration, let her down—her brothers, who stole her inheritance, her uncle's kids, who tried to steal it, her husband, who died young, and his greedy bully of a brother—but she got the better of them all and ended up richer than the lot of them. A hundred *faddan*s, and of the best land, which she bought with the sweat of her brow, and all that was left to dream for was the son who'd make it all worthwhile. And then my uncle Musa, the Raider's father, came—white, tall, and imposing, and of princely lineage for sure. But that's another story. Let's stick with the Raider.

By the time he left, or was forced out, he'd already tricked his way out of army service and got up to every kind of mischief. Theft, kidnapping, molesting girls, and anything else you can think of. He used to go to Fayoum City just to scare the girls. He loved girls and was very shy with them, but the only way he could think of to show his love and his shyness was, sad to say, to jump them. They'd be taken aback to find him jumping out at them stark naked, stiff as a poker from head to toe. Or a girl would wake up to find he'd climbed down from the roof and got into her room, or was pouncing on her from someplace like a real phantom raider.

Once he must have mixed "a bit of this with a bit of that" and happened to think of some inoffensive peasant from our village who'd "given him a dusty answer about something or refused him something when he wasn't stoned" and was overcome by a desire for vengeance that burned brighter with each toke and gulp. Or maybe it was some incredible pill that drove the Phantom Raider to pick up the jerry-can of kerosene and launch an attack on the inoffensive peasant's house (which was basically made of nothing but reed, palm fiber, and other incendiary materials) and set fire to it. When the fire caught, he came to his senses and realized what he'd done, and if he hadn't, and hadn't started yelling and banging on the doors of the houses in the middle of the night, our whole hamlet would have burned to the ground. This incident brought the Raider his first physical injury.

Everyone gathered and saw the disaster and he helped put it out from on top of the wall of the house. They were passing the water up to him in pots and pans without lids and he was flinging it over the fire with all his strength and zeal, his eyes closed, and then someone passed him up a jerry-can with the cap on and he flung it over the fire and it took him with it right into its middle and the skin on his legs broke out in blisters. But that didn't get in the way of his extraordinary ability to run, clamber, slither, and slide his way out of the clutches of any government in any country, with notable displays of these skills in three—Egypt, Libya, and Italy. In Egypt, in Danyal (district of Etsa, the Fayoum), Cairo, Alexandria, and Sharm el-Sheikh, as a fugitive, or a transient, or a returnee from Italy, failed, shamed, and without a clue what to do. In Libya, in Tobruk, Benghazi, el-Beida, Sirte, and Misrata. In Italy, in Lampedusa, Sicily, and Milan, with its forests and bustling waste lots.

Of course, the Raider wasn't a real thief, and there's no way he could have been, either before he went to Italy or after he came back. Think of his thefts as no more than youthful devilry, a phase usually undergone by those whose forefathers' glorious poetry praised their dashing exploits on horseback, plundering or robbing at knife point. Maybe young men are like that everywhere, loving to look tough and have a good time and with nothing against the odd grab-and-run to pay for food: "Just a quick grab to pay for something to get high on and a night out 'and, by the way, we accept cash!'" With him, though, it went on too long. He thought he could just go on playing the fool and jumping over walls into people's houses in the middle of the night. People began to fear him and find him intolerable. He couldn't even tolerate himself, and on top of all that the poverty and the big dreams (the "nice house with a northern breeze, the latest-model car, money to squander on those animals my relatives") so there was no obvious way out except to join the shit-gatherers. They alone the Phantom Raider left barefoot only to find them princes on his return.

There, in Italy, on the streets of Milan, the Raider was given, or gave himself, numerous names, one name for each stage of his life there. He entered Italy as Azam Abdallah Sfeit. He played the fool there as el-Baffo Saddam el-Masri, and he went to jail there as Diyab. And all these were over and above his official name Ihab and his nickname Muhyi.

The Attack

HE HELD US "IN STORAGE" in the desert. A house in the middle of the desert, the barren desert of Zuwara. Me, Muhammad el-Zaim, around a hundred and fifty Egyptians plus a few Pakistanis and Bangladeshis, the rest Africans from Ghana, Nigeria, Kenya. The house was large and had a wall, and we—us guys, the only Arabs—were in charge. Even the smugglers treated us like we were the camp leaders. The Pakistanis and the Bangladeshis lived in rooms off to the side and the Africans made little wooden huts next to the wall. We lived there for three months as prisoners. I mean real prisoners. We were told not even to look beyond the wall and the Libyan Auxiliary Police made the rocky hills around us shake while they searched for us, or for the house, specifically.

Being held in the pen is called being in storage, which means hiding out in the desert in preparation for the escape across the water. But every time we asked, they said, Soon! Fine, so when exactly? No one knew. One day I got sick of it and said, I'm going out, I'm going out. I'll play dumb the way I play dumb when I can't take it any more. So I took Muhammad el-Zaim and we went to Zuwara City, which was close, and we walked around in the streets and bought hashish and *bookha*, a kind of alcohol they make on the QT in the houses and farms.

Anyway, we got them and at night we came back. I went into the house and left the others to get everything ready in the main room and I took off my clothes. Then I went out barefoot and in my underwear to fill the jerry-can from the well outside in the courtyard. I heard a movement and noticed a shape. The main gate has an opening in it and when I got there I found myself staring at the face of a Libyan policeman, who screamed, Hold it, you son of a bitch! I looked and found another climbing over the gate and he shone a flashlight, *bam!*, in my face. Right away I made a break for it toward the Africans' huts and as I was running I saw one of them on top of the wall. Get down! Get down! the policeman shouted, and he cocked his automatic. The guys inside thought I was fighting the Africans—we were always fighting them—and ran out holding sticks and knives. I jumped on top of the wall then down the other side and landed, *bam!*, on the hood of the car belonging to the Auxiliary Police and sprinted off, and they sprinted after me.

I thought, It's over, you've got armed police chasing you in the desert, but it turned out they were pathetic—blacks, and scared. As I was running, I came across a corral full of sheep and goats—palm-rope netting with sheep and goats inside—and I threw myself into the middle of them. They fussed a bit, then settled down, and when the police arrived the old man who owned the animals went out to them and yelled, Who is it? They said, We're the Auxiliaries, the Auxiliary Police. He told them, Screw the Auxiliaries! What do you want? They said, A bunch of Egyptians escaped and one of them ran this way. He told them, Get out of here! Fuck off, Auxiliaries! You woke me for some pissy little Egyptian? Go on, get out of here, piss pants! And they turned right around while I lay there in the middle of the sheep and goats, rigid with fear. I'm like, If the guy can cuss out the government out like that, what's he going to do with me? The police left and the man stood there peering around for about an hour, scratching from time to time or stretching or farting or looking out into the darkness like a total idiot. The smell of the animals was terrible, and I was lying with the animals and sick to death of the animals. Finally he went inside, and when I felt sure he must have gone to sleep, I crawled on my belly through the animals and jumped out of the corral and sprinted off again.

I ran not less than five kilometers. It was night and every now and then when I saw the lights of the Auxiliaries' car as it roamed around I'd throw myself into a hollow. In the end, I found an olive farm with huge old olive presses from the time of the Italians. The moment I went in an army, a real army, of dogs rose up at me, not less than forty. I thought, That's it, I've been rumbled, I'm going to be eaten for dinner, and I set off running till I found a bowl, a kind of big hole. I looked down and saw a road, a fine road, running through it connecting Zuwara to el-Jmeil near the Tunisian border. Overlooking the road I found a half-finished brick hut, about two meters square, with a window onto the road. Never in my life have I been or will I ever again be as cold as I was there. I felt like someone was boring holes into my bones with a drill, and ordinary freezing cold—you know the freezing cold I mean?—as far as I was concerned that was comfort and warmth compared to the burning hell I was in. I stayed in the hut from ten o'clock at night till six o'clock in the morning, in the mountain cold. I couldn't lie down or stay still. I just jumped around, watching the police cars picking up Egyptians and Pakistanis and Africans who'd been held with me and tying their arms behind their backs and making them lie on the floors of the cars one on top of another in two layers and policemen in each car standing on top of them in their army boots and the beating and the insults without end and anyone who raised his head getting it punched right back down again with a rifle butt: You wanna to cross over to Italy, you son of a bitch? You wanna to cross over to Italy, you dog? Lie down, you pissy little Egyptian!

MIA in October and Almost
Finished Off by the Phantom Raider

THE FIRST THING THE PHANTOM Raider did was get himself
smuggled into Libya: "Somewhere to take cover till everyone
had forgotten about me and the mess I'd left behind." When
he got there, he was seduced by the dream of Italy, the gearshift that would make everything come out right, and he went
to stay with a relative of his who'd gone MIA during the Octo-
ber 73 War and in fact had been reported dead. We'd received
condolences for him but it turned out he'd deserted and gone
to a family in el-Sharqiya that had a mechanic's workshop and
had hidden there for three years before going off to Libya in
the time of the Leader, during the fuss about giving Egyptian
Bedouins Libyan nationality.

The Raider worked with him, probably mixing cement
for a builder, or plastering, in the building where his relation
was a guard or doing the finishing work. A four-story building
overlooking a house, or to be precise, the yard at the back of
a house, that belonged to a Libyan family—father, mother,
and four young daughters—and one day our MIA relation
found himself seized, a captive and surrounded by knives "till
you hand over that cousin of yours who's running wild, who
has offended our honor, and whom we have to kill." Eventually, he worked out that the Raider, whom he'd told them was
his cousin and from a big-shot family in Egypt, "had taken
his clothes off in the middle of the house and then stood on
the roof of the building stark naked with his legs spread" and

the four girls "had spent the whole day gawping up at him from below (meaning from *be-low be-low*—I don't know how to break up the word so that it's directly $^{\text{be-}}_{\text{low}}$ him)."

So, of course, the Raider ran away—running was basically his thing anyway—and then came back later to negotiate the salvation of his cousin from certain death and denied everything, even to the people who'd seen him with their own eyes. And the Libyans, being kindly folk, disbelieved their eyes but made it a condition that he go, and he left Sirte altogether and went to stay with a bunch of our relations in Misrata. That was probably where he met Muhammad el-Zaim el-Rumhi, who in Egypt had been just a distant relative but in Milan became like a first cousin, getting his back on everything: "He got my back so much he almost got himself killed at Balats 42, at the train station, and at the House of Abundance— and then there was the thing with the judge's computer, which almost did him in for real."

And, what with the extra-fine cigarettes and the *bookha*, humanity's dream (the gearshift, the house that would be better than some shit-collector's mansion, the latest-model car, the money that's enough so you don't have to work) came back to them ("and we accept cash by the way! A decent sum, enough for a couple or three generations so a guy can get some rest."). And there was no one quicker or crazier or more legendary, or I don't know what to say about or use to describe them, than the shit-collectors: the huts and animal sheds that were transformed into mansions of bricks and mortar and the money and the names—brilliant, rich, and successful in different professions and projects and even taking over entire major utilities in Milan and the rest of Italy, and there were so many of them, my friend. A whole Egyptian village transported to Italy! A whole quarter in the center of Milan called Tatoun! And they all came by the same route—the smuggler's, or better, the drowner's—from the coasts of Libya to the coasts of Italy.

And no sooner did the Phantom Raider and el-Zaim think about getting smuggled than a smuggler turned up! In fact, he'd been sitting with them anyway in the café at Suq el-Khamis in Misrata. Everyone knew the score. Goods on sale in the market, global pricing. And when it came to drowning, they were the lowest grade, the *terzo*, the "thirty thousand Egyptian pounds that the smuggler takes half of now, with your passport as guarantee for the other half and to be returned to your family in Egypt when they pay and you hand yourself over to him"-type. Confiscating the passports has another advantage. It makes it easy for the smuggled person to claim, on appearing before the Italian authorities, the nationality of any crisis-stricken or war-torn Arab country, such as Palestine or Iraq. The Raider chose Iraq and gave himself the name of his smuggler, Azam Abdallah Sfeit.

Suq el-Khamis

EL-ZAIM, MIDA BU GHALEB, MUHAMMAD el-Nayed, Ahmad from Roufan, Saleh and his brother Alloum from the Laaraj family, and another kid from Minyet el-Heit, all of them Bedouin from the Fayoum, were with me. We stayed in Suq el-Khamis for about two weeks and met up again with my friends, the thugs. They were from the biggest family in the market, and they were putting the market, along with the whole area, through hell with their thefts and kidnappings. They introduced me to a new smuggler called Azam Abdallah Sfeit, saying, This is the guy who gets people over to Italy. First he put us in storage at his coffee-shop in Zuwara till there were enough of us. He had a bossy Sudanese with him so we taught him a lesson. He was very tall and strong and he lorded it over us, especially the Egyptians, like he was a Libyan when he was just a filthy servant. He kept saying, You pissy little Egyptian! You Egyptian donkey! so me and El-Zaim grabbed him and wiped the floor with him and from that day on he licked our boots and even Azam was scared.

He had two prostitutes from Tunis at the coffee-shop. They served drinks and slept in two rooms at the side. If you liked one, you'd sweeten her up with a hundred dinars, do it with her in the room, and come out. She wasn't the first one I'd slept with. Once I raped a woman in the Fayoum. It wasn't real rape, don't get me wrong. She was from our hamlet and had married someone in another hamlet and I'd never looked at her and she wasn't pretty at all, very skinny, just skin and bones, and I lay in wait for her in the fields, where the big animal sheds are. Anyway, it doesn't matter, friend—the funny thing is she was the first woman I saw after I got back from Italy. The Tunisian girl, though, was the first and last I wanted to live with for the rest of my life. She liked men, men themselves. She wasn't the type who sits there complaining and makes you feel bad. She'd tell you she did what she did because she liked it: I like to make a man happy. Her eyes were yea big and that's the most beautiful thing there is.

At the back of the coffee-shop there was a tunnel that went down, a kind of ramp that opened onto a large basement underneath the café. That was where we slept. We stayed there a week and a new group came that wanted to make the journey and there got to be lots of us in the coffee-shop. I tried every trick I knew with Azam to allow us to take the Tunisian girl with us and let me look after her but no way.

Tatoum

IN THE MIDDLE OF THE Bedouin settlements in the southern Fayoum, there's a hamlet called Tatoun, which is peasants but surrounded on all sides by Bedouin, and I think it's Tatoun—or the nearby hamlet of Khalil el-Gindi—that boasts to all the other hamlets in the area that "There isn't a single Bedouin or Christian here!" The poor peasants of Tatoun used to collect the Arabs' wastes—our personal body wastes, not the wastes of the animals and the ordinary garbage.

In those days, and perhaps even now, the Bedouin would relieve themselves "on the mound." Their animals relieved themselves in the fields and houses and they did so "on the mound." The first freedom the rural desert-dweller loses in the city is that he can't do it on the mound, and I myself suffered greatly from this when I first came to Cairo. It's a shocking thing, doing it on the mound, but it's an ancient, ingrained custom imposed by the desert's particular situation, its hard-scrabble life, its freedom, and, of course, its Bohemianism. As you will be of course aware, Lady A'isha, the Prophet's wife, was falsely accused of having sexual relations with Safwan ibn Muattal when she was relieving herself "on the mound."

The people of Tatoun used to collect their merchandize in big burlap sacks that they placed on the donkeys and filled, using large baskets made of palm fronds. Despite their poverty, both their baskets and their donkeys were taller, stronger, and larger than our hamlet's baskets and donkeys, and they themselves were healthier, cleaner, and more energetic than our hamlet's peasants. When the sack was full, they'd turn the basket upside down on top of it and the shit-gatherer would "hop up on top and sit there, lolling about like he was on a king's throne." They used it to manure the few acres of vegetables and other crops they had, which they then sold to the Bedouin themselves at the Saturday market in Tatoun and the Wednesday market in el-Gharg, life thus coming full circle, the Bedouin eating and defecating, the Tatounis collecting and selling, extolling the stuff's strength as vegetable fertilizer, and the Bedouin, of course, eating—I mean like really eating—and being lazy and not liking to work. In other words, "finding one of their whoppers was like a holiday for the overworked Tatouni, who ran around all day chasing after a turd here and a turd there."

Then Italy suddenly hove into view, and the children of the shit-gatherers travelled, or to be more precise took sail, or to be even more precise, survived drowning, and came back as emperors, I mean like real emperors—villas, mansions, money, and huge success, here and in Italy. Two of the Phantom Raider's friends, of the same generation and age, were Tatounis—one the owner of the biggest scaffolding company in the whole of Milan, the other the owner of the agency for maintaining apartment block façades for the whole of Milan.

They all flocked to Milan, where they were considered a recognized foreign community, or at least a group of note. Some of them lived like the Raider, in vacant lots and forests and abandoned castles. Some lived in apartments. And the ones the Lord saw fit to bless, in a house with a whole hamlet around it, like the brothers who converted a historic government building into an entire hamlet in the middle of the forest. The ones on the wrong side of the law had their headquarters, or their best-known settlement, in the "Balats" in the center of Milan, otherwise known as Building 42 and celebrated among drug dealers, policemen, and outlaws in general throughout the city to this day. Once the police raided Balats 42 while the Raider was staying in an apartment there with a buddy. They had two kilos of heroin on them and while they were waiting for the police, who were at the door, "they spread the two kilos out between them in the bathroom and set to, swallowing it by the handful till they passed out."

The Rabbit Farm

HE MOVED US TO HIS farm in the desert, around a hundred and fifty hectares with an enclosure in the middle and a rabbit-raising operation, a large trench about five meters deep, three wide, and three hundred long, all rabbits and rabbit burrows. At night, the ground was covered with rabbits but the moment you looked at them they vanished. Azam, despite his money, or because of it, was a miser and fed us one meal a day, which came at night, so we were always hungry. So I stayed up all night and made a plan. At dawn, when everything was fresh and quiet, the rabbits would come out of the burrows, leave the trench entirely and move around in the olive garden for about an hour, then go back before sunrise, so I got the whole group ready, about thirty-five men, and we stayed up all night next to the trench and at half past three the rabbits began coming out of their burrows bunch after bunch till there were about seventy of them. Then we blocked the burrows—stuff stuff stuff!—with rice straw. There weren't a lot of burrows but underground they were like streets and tunnels. Some of us went to the forest to round up the rabbits there and others waited down below in the trench, and the rabbits came running, searching for the burrows and not finding them. But some of them knew where they were and stuck their heads through the straw and in, and in, and maybe six others would go in after them. Still, we caught a few and slaughtered them, skinned them, cleaned out the guts, and grilled them over the fire. We kept this up for around a month till the rabbits got too scared to come out of their burrows even to eat or drink.

Azam Abdallah Sfeit was a Berber and spoke Arabic, Berber, and Italian. He was twenty-six years old but if you saw him you'd say fifty—tall, fat, white, and with flowing locks. He had backers, not like the smuggler before him. He knew people in the Libyan government. He had a brother called el-Zentani who was on the run from a twenty-five-year prison sentence for a smuggling case, but "on the run" was just on paper— he went everywhere like normal and if any of the people in storage was arrested, he'd go to the police and get him out; it was no big deal. In any case, smuggling, as far as our brother Libyans and the Bedouin in general were concerned, wasn't a crime or a job to be ashamed of, it was heroic, and when you asked one of them, What's your work? he'd tell you with great pride, I'm in smuggling, just like the Bedouin used to boast in the old days that they stole and plundered, because it was thought of like chivalry. Azam had good contacts with the Libyan government and police force and his father was one of those who'd joined the revolution with Muammar el-Gaddafi on the 1st of September. When he said something, people did what he said, and when he went into the police station, they'd say, Hajj Sfeit's here! Once the police raided us in an almost finished apartment block where they were storing us temporarily and they phoned him and he came after they'd put us into the trucks and the moment the officer saw him they took us down straight away and apologized to Hajj Sfeit.

One day Azam came and moved us to a new farm close to the sea and that was where we set off from on the journey where I saw death with my own eyes. We were forty Egyptians and two Tunisians and they put us in a wooden boat but Azam didn't check the weather forecast. We just got on and set off. We sailed all night and by the time we got to the Bouri oilfield at the far side of Libyan waters in the morning a strong wind had risen and the sea had gotten rough and the waves had turned into real mountains. You'd see one coming toward you and it would raise the boat till you could see a canyon in front of you and a canyon behind you and then it would bring the boat down till we thought the sea had swallowed us for good and then it would take you up again. Have you seen the guys who do surfing when a wave curls over them? That was our boat. The wave would roar and raise the boat till we felt like it was flying and then bring it crashing down into the bowels of the sea, and by the time we'd bobbed up again, another catastrophe would be heading for us. The kids were bailing water out of the boat, some saying, There is no god but God, some praying, some saying, I swear I'm going to piss myself, which they did. It was a shambles and there were crying and voices yelling, Lord! Lord! and everyone thought they were going to die. I sat there and didn't do anything. I just sat where I was and waited for death. Everyone around me was yelling and crying and I sat there saying nothing and telling myself, When the boat sinks I'll swim. I know how to swim and all the time I'm swimming I'll say, There is no god but God. If I get eaten I get eaten and if I make it I make it. And then, all of a sudden, we found ourselves beneath the pillars of the Bouri oil platform. It stands on ten, each the size of a large house, an enormous iron-sheathed concrete tube holding up the platform over our heads. We saw men looking down at us so we yelled to them, Throw something to us! Please throw us some rope or something so we can shin up it! But nothing. They left us to our deaths and disappeared. We went on wrestling with the sea all day long and whenever a wave came we'd think, This is it, the sea's going to swallow us now, till we found a huge dredger bearing down on us going *tawoo-oo-oo*! We waved to them so they came closer and told us, Calm down! Stop moving about and we'll rescue you, and they threw us a rope and we tied it to the prow of the boat and the dredger towed us all the way till it handed us over to the Tunisian lifeguards. They asked us, Where are you from?—Egyptians! Making for where?—Italy! So they said, As you're Egyptians and brothers, we won't arrest you, we'll take you back to Libya, and they took us to an area called the Salt Flats, on the Libyan coast, and waved us off toward the east saying, Libya's over there and as soon as you get out of the Salt Flats you'll find yourselves at the road that leads to el-Jmeil. Then they left us.

The Leader

SALEH BU HABBOUNA THE LIBYAN is the same person as Saleh
Bu Habbouna the Egyptian, from the Mashrigi tribe. When he
went to Libya, they identified him as belonging to his mother's
husband's tribe, to which the Leader also belonged, and even
though he didn't like his mother's husband and had a particular
hatred for the Leader and his tribe, he joined it. They told him,
"At least you can live off them!" Truly said, for to belong to the
Leader's tribe in the country the Leader ruled was to find that
all doors opened before one and all difficulties melted away.

Saleh was a poor Mashrigi Bedouin who'd been living
with his mother in the village of Outer Atiya, in the south of
the Fayoum. He had worked as a servant with his father in the
headman's house, and when the headman died and the headmanship was lost to the family, the inheritance was divided
up. He ended up as part of the sons' share and couldn't even
afford to feed himself, so he went to Libya in the seventies.

He was seventeen and went "under the wire" with the
smugglers' donkeys. First Salloum, then the march of seventeen kilometers into the desert hidden among the donkeys
carrying the smuggled goods, and he crossed the wire and
arrived at Musaed along with a group of his neighbors and
two of his relations.

Immediately, they gave him papers as a Libyan Saad-Shin
"returnee" from the Leader's tribe and he worked in a construction company with the now celebrated Bedouin praise-caller

and master of wedding ceremonies Bu Gargour and the even more celebrated singer Awad Bu Abd el-Gader el-Malki, who were both seventeen-year-olds like him. One day, five armored cars from the Libyan army arrived and took him, along with the singer, Bu Gargour and all the other Saad-Shins who were working in the company, of whom there were forty, counting everyone, some with and some without educational qualifications, and enrolled them in the Libyan army, at a training center from hell where they stayed for three months. They graduated at a military ceremony attended by the Leader himself. They took the names of the kids who were from his tribe and seconded them to his personal guard at el-Aziziya, his permanent headquarters, the place where he uttered his last cry before being murdered. The rest they distributed among the Saad-Shin companies fighting in the Sahara at Aouzou. The Leader preferred and trusted the Saad-Shin troops and held them up to the Libyan troops as examples of fortitude, excellence, dedication, and devotion to soldiering, so as to shame them.

While they were being transported through the desert that stretches between Sirte, where the training camp was located, and Sabha, which was the forward position for the fighting in Aouzou, the singer, Awad Bu Abd el-Gader el-Malki, escaped. He escaped and went back to Egypt, where his days of glory as an artist began. Saleh was inducted into the Leader's guard at el-Aziziya. He was part of the regular guard, who wore military uniforms and berets and were used as decoration, standing with their weapons at the main gate. Some of the Saad-Shin held high rank and were colonels and important commanders, like Colonel el-Rifi, a Rumhi from the Fayoum by origin, who liberated Aouzou. Saleh, having no education, was an ordinary soldier but he had the right to open fire on anyone who entered el-Aziziya without permission from the Leader, even if it was the Leader's own deputy. It was on this authority that Saleh Bu Habbouna joined the rest of the guard in firing on the officer Hasan Ashkal and killing him.

Ashkal was an officer close to the Leader, belonged to his tribe, and had previously been a plainclothes policeman in Sabha. When the mighty 1st of September revolution arose, the Leader transferred him to the army and made him a commander of the forces positioned around his birthplace of Sirte. Nobody knows why he was killed at the gate of el-Aziziya.

The Zodiac

SUDDENLY WE FOUND OURSELVES SURROUNDED by Libyan police cars, so we shot off, different bunches going different ways and scattering through the desert. El-Zaim and I kept on running till we came to a tent and someone watching over some sheep and goats, so we went and told him, We're Egyptians on the run from the police. Please protect us! so he went into the tent and came out again with two *galabiya*s and two pairs of drawers and head wraps and said, Get out of those clothes and put these on and pretend to be looking after the animals, and we barely had time for each of us to grab a stick and start rounding up the sheep and goats before the police caught up with us. The man stood his ground in front of them and said, What's up? What do you want? and they said, The Gypos, and he said, Fuck off! There aren't any Gypos here, and he pointed to us and said, Those are my brother's boys and they're working with me. Fuck off the both of you! and the police fucked off.

We stayed with the man till the late afternoon. Then we went down to the road to el-Jmeil and waved down a guy driving a Peugeot. He guessed we were on the run from the authorities, took double the fare, and drove us to Zuwara and from Zuwara to Suq el-Khamis. We stayed at Suq el-Khamis for about a month and Azam got in touch with us and put us in storage in a house with a Libyan family. There were around forty of us and we stayed locked up in one room night and day, like in a prison, for six months. In the mornings young children would come and open the door for us and we'd walk up and down the corridor and go back to the room. One day Azam phoned us and said, The authorities are coming for you. Run, now! You have exactly ten minutes before the police raid the house looking for you. So all forty of us began banging on the door, banging on the door, banging on the door, and by the time the owner of the house heard us and opened it, the police had arrived. They arrested us and took us to the Zuwara police station (and now comes a bit you'll really get a kick out of, lads!).

They took us inside one by one for questioning before going into the lock-up, and the moment anyone went inside all we'd hear was screams. When I went in, I saw right off that there was someone behind the door and he gave me a smack, *whop!*, on the back of my neck with his hand and the moment I turned around there was another one who gave me a thwack, *whap!*, on the same place. I was just straightening up when someone else went *bam!*, right on my ear and it was like, You wanna to cross over to Italy, you pissy little Egyptian? and the beating continued.

We were Bedouin from different Egyptian tribes but we all spoke like Egyptians, except one guy called Bu el-Neid who was from the same district as me in the Fayoum, from the settlement at el-Sarira, who could only speak Bedouin. The western Libyan police thought he must be a Mashrigi Bedouin, in other words an enemy from Benghazi pretending to be Egyptian. Glory be, what a tough bastard he showed himself to be that night! Every half-hour they'd open the door of the lock-up and ask, Where's the Mashrigi? then take him and beat him to the point of death and bring him back gasping for breath. I'd say, Bu el-Neid! Bu el-Neid! Talk like an Egyptian, Bu el-Neid! and he'd tell me, Ah cain't! It's the way me tongue is! They'd leave him to rest for a while, and then it'd be, Come along, Mashrigi! till the morning.

And in the morning, it was, like, Let's go! We're taking you to Hawwazet el-Enab—which was a prison built by the Italians in Misrata and known as a place of violent death. They'd pull out your fingernails, sit you on a bottle, electrocute you, and fuck you all day and all night. They took us out of the lock-up and it was like, Let him have it! Let him have it! from one hand to another till we were nearly dead and then it was like, Halt the bus! Back it up! Load the little pissers up! A car set off behind us but on the highway it went in front with two armed soldiers in the back and two next to the driver, plus there were two with us on the bus, each with an automatic. El-Zaim and I sat at the back to get away from the beating and the cussing out, and when we got to the desert I noticed the window next to me could be opened and I wedged my back against it and pushed and it opened, so I said to him, Zaim! Zaim! I'm going to jump, then as soon as the bus slowed down, I put my legs through, squeezed myself together hard, pulled in my head, grabbed onto the glass with my hands, straightened my legs and rested my weight on the fender, and before the bus could pick up speed again I found myself on my belly in the desert with el-Zaim behind me. We shot off through the desert and by the time they realized what had happened, they were far away and we'd made it into the desert. We hid with a Bedouin sheikh who was herding sheep and goats and worked for him for two days.

Then we set out for Misrata and stayed in a place called Four Corners where we found a bunch of the Sarira boys who'd been in storage with us at Zuwara. We stayed with them for about four months, then went back to Suq el-Khamis and met Azam and he took us to the new storage place, on the outskirts of Zuwara, in an almost finished villa that belonged to him and where we were supposed to be laborers.

There were fifteen of us—the rest they took to the rabbit farm—and we stayed there for about three months. One day a police car arrived and a black officer got out all puffed up and with a few soldiers around him, but the moment he found out it was Hajj Abdallah Sfeit's villa and we were his workers, he shriveled up, he was so scared. He said, Okay, okay, and turned his car round and left again. We called Azam and he went and gave them a dressing-down at the police station: How—how exactly—could you raid the villa and terrorize my workers? Have you gone crazy? I'm taking you to the Leader right this minute!—like the Leader was sitting there waiting for someone to beat the living daylights out of.

One day, Azam turned up looking anxious and told us to get ready for the journey. A car came and took us to a storage pen near the sea where there were people from every country—more than fifty Egyptians and about a hundred Africans, not to mention the Pakistanis and the Indians and the Bangladeshis. Azam stood in the middle of us and said, Listen up, everyone! All I've got now is a Zodiac. The boat that's going to Italy is a Zodiac. (A Zodiac is an inflatable dinghy with a 50 h.p. engine that only takes five passengers, though they put forty in it.) Will you go, you Egyptians? They said, No, we agreed on a wooden boat. So he asked the Africans and they said, No, and the Pakistanis, No, and the Indians, No, and the Bangladeshis, Okay. There were exactly forty of them, and he turned to me and el-Zaim and he said, Will you go? and we said, We'll go. Of course, the other Egyptians were saying, Have you gone nuts, son? You'll die, son. You'll drown, son. A Zodiac's just air, son, and it gets punctures at sea. But I'd made up my mind—I'm going means I'm going.

El-Zaim and I set off with Azam in a truck we'd loaded with the army-camouflaged Zodiac, along with the wooden parts and the engine, and took it to the shore behind a high dune. Then we laid out the Zodiac, put the wooden slats into the floor and sides, closed the zippers, inflated it, and mounted the engine on the back. We put in twenty jerry-cans of water, twenty of gasoline, and ten cartons of pressed dates. There were six Libyans, plus me and Azam, who had brought around twenty Pakistanis to help, and we lifted the Zodiac and put it into the sea. The driver, Rashid el-Tunsi, came, and when it got dark, Azam brought the forty Bangladeshis and told me, You and el-Zaim are in charge of the Zodiac, along with the driver. Three Libyans stood in the Zodiac and began pulling the Bangladeshis in one by one and with every pull they cleaned them out, one hand grabbing his hand and the other his wallet—if you're being smuggled you mustn't have anything on you but your clothes and the money. El-Zaim and me and the driver got in. We had two plastic bags of *bookha* with us and two sticks of hashish. The Zodiac took off with Azam on board, and after about a kilometer he said, Off you go, then! Happy landings! and dived into the sea.

The Omelet and
Meat-and-Potatoes Restaurant

My mother probably gave me too much rein. She needed a man and I was there, so she decided I was one. From the moment my father died, when I was five, she treated me as though I was her husband. Sex excepted, we conducted our daily life as though she was the strong, sensible wife and I the honest, obedient husband. When I compare her strength as a widow and my fear for my own children now, I'm amazed. From the time I was in Preparatory, she'd let me go off to Cairo to work and be away for two or three weeks with complete confidence. She'd send me to irrigate the fields in the depths of the night and sleep on the threshing floor when I was still a child in Elementary. From my side, I was well broken in and wherever she threw me I stuck, like a leech. I'd hoe a half-hectare or work as a day laborer, and my great joy, and even greater sense of fulfilment, came from handing over to her every cent I earned.

But it wasn't enough for a lady of Bedouin, or even peasant, origins. "Kids go abroad. Go abroad, son! I want to see you with a child before I die." We had our half-hectare of land and our donkey and our cow and our dog and the butter ball straight from the churn to guzzle on and a guest parlor that we'd fill with enough grain for a year. All the same, she began to worry over my still being there, and even more over Cairo, or my going to Cairo. "Some strange woman will take him away and I won't see him again. Go abroad, son! All the kids have gone abroad and worked and brought back money, and I'm getting old and want to see you with a child before I die."

And as soon as I got to Libya, I beheld the tragedy of it all: "the Heavens and the Morning-star." A sandbox, as Mussolini said. Add to which the incident in Benghazi, when the crazy officer shook us down, and that there's nothing to do but stand in the marketplace and throw yourself, along with the rest of the army of Egyptian laborers, at any Libyan, who usually wants just one worker to mow barley in the barren desert. I tried once to get a job in journalism but all I met with was empty promises. *1st of September* and *The Green March*, the only two papers in Sabha as well as the whole of the rest of Libya, basically had nobody working for them. In Sabha, the wind whistled through their offices. Anyway, I'd never believed wholly or finally that I'd really be able to work as a journalist in Libya. It's also a fact that the only time I was ever able to work as a journalist was when I was bored during the off-season at Bu el-Helb's workshop and I had a Bedouin friend from the Fayoum who was a poet, a graduate of el-Azhar, and the son of a long-time and important Saad-Shin. Together we wrote a poem in praise of the Leader, hoping it might make us a little money, and we recited it together out loud in the streets of Sabha as we returned empty-handed from the offices of *The Green March* and were going up the red-dirt slope at the start of the industrial quarter. It was a literal transposition of some of the sayings of the Leader in his *Green Book* and from his Third International Theory: "Those who form parties are but traitors to the Covenant, unfaithful to their trust!" which was a transposition of, or inspired by, the saying, "Those who form parties are traitors," which was written in bold font in *The Green Book* and on every street in Libya for the benefit of the current generation and was even said to be written on the bed of the Mediterranean for the benefit of those to come.

Anyway, I could have gone back. Egypt was far better. Even our own field, if well farmed, would have been better. But it never crossed my mind to go back.

I worked for a time in a restaurant at the workshop that belonged to el-Hasnawi, a Libyan, for its tenant, Hadi, a Tunisian, then for a time as a body painter's assistant, and eventually making cement blocks. The fact that I left the restaurant during an absurd battle and nearly got killed painting trucks is irrelevant. The truth is that I liked the independence of block-making and the field was wide open ("The sky's the limit!") and doing it was "a thing about which there was no doubt" (as it says in the Good Book), not to mention that it was easy. Not something that demanded no effort, of course. On the contrary, it was exhausting, but it was easy. The block-making machine consisted of an iron box containing a moving iron press with an iron cover on top attached to an iron support with an iron arm, or plunger, or plate, that descended on the iron box containing the mixture. The cover was removed and the press came down and extruded a block of the required size.

Unfortunately, though, it turned out that things weren't that simple and that it was a profession with rules and aspects to it, and that enthusiasm without knowledge was, sorry to say, a killer. The masters of the cement-block trade in Sabha were Levantines—the Syrians for making the blocks, while their gurus, and I would even go so far as to say their masters, were the Lebanese, who made the machines that made the blocks. I hadn't studied at all, either with the Lebanese or the Syrians. I thought it was all a matter of physical strength and endurance. Perhaps because of my naivety, or my Bedouin features, or the honesty that welled from my eyes, an officer in the Libyan army decided to take a chance on me and made me a deal—50,000 blocks for a plant to be built by the Libyan army. I wish to God I'd never made them or sold them. The blocks fell to pieces in the hands of the soldiers who came to put them into the trucks and I would have gone to jail except that the blocks were for the Libyan army, where things were worked out—along the lines of the officer's being my friend and a faithful customer of Bu Abdallah's and "this poor kid's got nothing but the shirt on his back."

The industrial quarter is at the beginning of Sabha on the road to the airport. On its corner there was a chicken restaurant, which I think is still there. It was the restaurant patronized by the quarter's big shots, the workshop owners and older skilled workers. The hired laborers, junior workers, and various helpers, on the other hand, ate at my place, in the restaurant at the run-down workshop.

The soil of the industrial quarter is red and it begins with a brick-red slope that makes you think you must be in Africa, though people with dusky skins and African features are not in the majority in Sabha. On the contrary, it's the refuge and hometown of the Saad-Shin Bedouin, who aren't originally Libyan in origin but Egyptian citizens forced by circumstances to work in Libya. Now, as I've told you, there are three levels of Egyptians working abroad—the smart guys, who go to Europe, the middling, who go to Iraq and the Gulf, and the completely clueless types with no educational qualifications and no profession, who go to Libya.

Maybe it was the color, plus the accent, the heat, the too-close sun, the blocks of cement, but in Sabha I felt a kind of laziness, or insensitivity, or indifference, or something of that sort. I have no idea why, but I associate the laziness and sluggishness that overcame me there with the sight of the abandoned Palace of Culture—a grand cultural palace equipped with theaters and truly towering performance spaces, and surrounded by an extensive garden, all built by the Leader to display culture and the arts and turned into a ruin, or not exactly a ruin but a meadow for fodder-cutters, the plants sprouting through the boards of the stage. I'm talking about my time there, in the seventies, not now, since the Palace of Culture must for sure have been plundered or blown to smithereens, and the garden that was full of trees on which camels grazed become a camp for some armed revolutionary group.

Anyway, Bu Abdallah and I rented a cement-block factory in the industrial quarter. When I first arrived, I stayed at Sabha airport, maybe in a wooden trailer for the airport workers, and from there I went to Bu Abdallah's. It might have been the cousin whom I went to stay with who introduced me to him, but I think it was the restaurant that brought us all together—me and Bu Abdallah and the Saad-Shin gang.

At the restaurant I also became friends with, and debated and quarreled with, Abd el-Aziz and Abd el-Slam, both Moroccans, Abd el-Aziz short and dusky and a Berber, a mechanic who knew more about Peugeots than their French manufacturers did, and Abd el-Slam, tall and fair-skinned and an Arab and no less of a genius than his fellow countryman when it came to panel beating. They both worked at the workshop with the guy who rented it, Hadi the Tunisian, and when I arrived and began cooking in its restaurant, they were my first customers. They drank moonshine and every Thursday night they'd hire Chadian whores, with their dark red complexions, towering height, and stare-you-down eyes, and sleep with them at the workshop.

Once Bu Abdallah brought a woman and put her to work, or was going to. I didn't know anything about it when he brought her to the factory's living quarters. She was from Ghana and had very soft and flabby breasts. When I fondled them as she stood submissively, or perhaps exhaustedly, in front of me, I found them as soft, or maybe as slack, as spent balloons. Unfortunately, those were the first breasts I'd touched so far in my life and maybe they're the ones that left me with the obsession that has driven me crazy for the rest of it. Anyway, I had no mercy on her. In those days to me she was the devil incarnate. "Fine, but even if she was, my friend, did that give you the right to make assumptions about her?"

Anyway, the only thing I could see in her was the devil. The girl was a fallen woman and I asked her disapprovingly, "What brings you here?"

Haughtily and with true contempt she replied, "*Wurrrk.* I've come here to *wurrrk.*" Then she added, in Arabic both clear and deeply felt, "Exactly like you."

I used to launch myself on Abd el-Aziz and Abd el-Slam and show them the path of true Islam via sermons and reproaches and never-ending boring warnings of the hellfire into which they would be thrown, where as soon as one of their skins was well done it would be replaced with another. Abd el-Aziz, the spokesman confident in his debauchery, insisted for a while that alcohol wasn't a sin, as proved by the noble verse of the Qur'an that says of wine, "Avoid it . . ." of which he'd say that "If our Lord meant 'Leave it alone altogether,' he would have said so clearly." The Chadian women he justified by saying that they were essentially concubines: "I invoke the analogy to concubines, my friend! I buy the girl at night and sell her in the morning."

They gave up arguing, though, when I moved into the factory. To be honest, they stopped arguing because I became a sinner too. Not a sinner once and for all, of course. You might say I became a sinner at the level of daily life, of the rules I followed, the people I was around and my fear of the authorities, not at the level of belief. I was as I have always been: an innocent among the wicked. I declared that alcohol was sinful but was around it and carried it about and sold it by the liter (one liter for ten dinars). Think of me as being like the family of Yaser—"Patience, O Family of Yaser!"—but without their sufferings or being forced like they were. No big deal—I fell into the clutches of a gang, the dregs of the Saad-Shin criminals created by the Leader and Commander . . . but that's another story.

Let's stick to the factory to begin with. It consisted of living quarters, that is, a room built of cement blocks and roofed with tin sheeting that grew flaming hot in the summer, plus an area of about a quarter of a hectare, with bathrooms at the back and in the middle the block-making machine, of which there was just one at first till I bought a second from the Lebanese guy. The blocks themselves were partly spread out in the drying area and partly stacked for transportation, while the gravel and sand were to the side. Finally, there was the stack of cement, right next to the living quarters so it wouldn't get stolen.

The *sharshur*, or gravel, and the sand were brought to me by a Mauritanian driver, who had a large Fiat truck. Riding with him and going to fetch the *sharshur* from the rock-breaker deep in the red mountains and returning covered all over with fine red dust was one of my rare pleasures in Sabha.

Lampedusa

WE ROSE IN THE DARK, the dark that's black as a shroud, as people say. Azam had told us that all we had to do was to "keep the compass between zero and one." The Zodiac bounced and bounced and there was nothing to hear but *chakk! chakk! chakk!* El-Zaim, the driver, and I were drinking *bookha* and smoking hashish at the front of the Zodiac next to the compass, and the Bangladeshis were sitting around the edge praying to the Lord and reading the Qur'an. Sometimes I'd drive, sometimes el-Zaim, sometimes Rashid, but all you got from the Bangladeshis was, God is great! God is great! I bear witness that there is no god but God!

When morning came we found nothing but water in all directions, and the sky *bluuuue* and so clear. The Zodiac forged ahead and after a little we found that the water had turned black and we saw dolphins leaping all around us and me and El-Zaim were wasted. It was August and we were all wearing just shorts, and we said to Rashid, Stop and let's have a swim, so he stopped the boat and we jumped into the sea while the Bangladeshis died of fright.

We got out and around afternoon prayer time we caught a far-off glimpse of buildings to our right—apartment blocks, houses, gardens. I said to them, That's Lampedusa over there! I have very good eyesight and Azam had told us, Sixteen hours and you'll be in Lampedusa. We sang songs praising the Zodiac—We made it! We made it! We made it!—and ripped out the compass, threw overboard the loudspeaker, the dates, and anything else that could prove we were coming from Libya, and set course for Lampedusa. After driving for about three hours, we found that "Lampedusa" was a giant ship, as big as Libya itself, with six large boats hanging from its side, and we had no food and no compass to guide us and no loudspeaker to hail anybody. Just us and the sea.

When we got close to the ship we saw Arabic writing on it. People came out to look at us and it was clear they were Tunisians. Rashid told them, We're refugees going to Lampedusa and we got lost on the sea.

They told us, Keep the Zodiac in a line with the ship and keep going straight, no left or right, and you'll find yourselves in Lampedusa. And make it real quick because in exactly four hours it's going to get rough. After about three hours we came across a boat full of Africans, families and small children, and they waved their jerry-cans at us and shouted, Gas! Gas! but we paid them no attention. While we were going at top speed, the Zodiac got a puncture, so we cut some empty gasoline jerry-cans open and made the Bangladeshis bail water. We kept going for eight hours and still no Lampedusa. We were lost at sea and night was coming. We got confused and stopped for a while, then went on, a little this way, a little that, but nothing. I thought, If the sea gets rough, I'm just going to dive into the water and get it over with.

Sicily

SUDDENLY, ABOUT A HALF-HOUR BEFORE sunset, a large helicopter hovered above us for ten minutes. We called out to it a lot, in all the languages Rashid knew, but it left. We chased after it but we were so flummoxed we forgot about the gas and the engine ran out and started to smoke. We put it out, put in more gas, and tried to start the engine but it wouldn't catch. Kaput, boss. And the sea, which had been smooth as a carpet, began to rise. We unfastened the engine so we could fix it and started fiddling with it on the edge of the Zodiac. It slipped out of our hands and slid into the sea. Gone. We watched it as it rolled over on its way down. Some cried, some screamed, and some said, There is no god but God. Suddenly we found some goddam awful thing right in front of us, with two helicopters on its back, about seven big guns, and pointing a big light at us. We turned round and found a second and a third. They formed a circle around us. There was some distance between us and them. They spoke English first, then Italian, then Arabic, through a megaphone. They said, We know you're refugees. Calm down and hand yourselves over because in a quarter of an hour the sea's going to get rough and you'll drown. One ship produced a great shower of soap, and we yelled. We were afraid they were going to kill us, but the voice said in Arabic, Don't be scared, it's disinfectant. Five minutes later the first ship turned on the spot and left and then the others suddenly disappeared over the sea and a small boat came. When we looked, we saw the

Maltese flag, so we refused to get off and said, We want Italy, not Malta. Malta would have sent us back to Egypt without question because it has an agreement with Egypt to return all fugitives, but Italy and the rest of Europe don't. We kept yelling, Italy, *yes*! Malta, *no*! and then the voice said it was a Maltese boat but it belonged to Italy, and we were now in Italian waters. We didn't want to but there was no way around getting on board with them. The Zodiac itself had begun to get heavy with water, and the moment we got on board with them, the sea got rough, with waves like mountains, and we reached the Red Cross in Lampedusa.

The moment we got down from the boat, everyone was received by two men and a girl—all looking very clean and wearing shiny suits, masks, and gloves, like they were about to handle scorpions. Then it was like, Take off your clothes, so we took off our clothes and were left wearing our underpants and they sent us in one by one to a desk where a male and a female doctor (blonde hair, very cute) were sitting. When you go in, she tells you, Come closer and pull your pants all the way down, and she examines your thing and your balls and feels you all over to see if anything's broken or there are any injuries. Then she tells you, Pull your pants up, and you go to the showers so they can rub you with disinfectant powder and you can wash. Then they hand you pajamas, rubber flip-flops, pants, a T-shirt, a blanket, a pillow, a sheet, and a mattress, and they go with you to the bed that's going to be yours in the dormitory. There was a tall Sudanese with us. The moment the doctor pulled his underpants down and looked at his thing, she said, Wow! She had this gadget with her, a black gadget kind of thing, and she spoke to her male colleague and it turned out that one of their female colleagues was looking for someone with a big thing, so they called her and she came and she was hot—a real looker, I mean—and she looked at the Sudanese guy's thing and said, Wow! Then she patted him on the shoulder and took him off to the bathroom in front of us all, like it was quite normal.

Up to then, I was still afraid that maybe it wasn't Italy. I was just this weird kid, you know, who thought that if he could make it to Italy he'd find everything was different and he'd have money and everyone would respect him. Italy was my only hope of going back to Egypt a millionaire. We went into the dormitory at the RC and I made my bed and went to wash the powder off. As I was standing in line waiting my turn, I looked over at the other showers and saw someone I knew from the Fayoum. His name was Ahmad Bu Naasa and he told me not to worry, I was in Italy.

We stayed at the Lampedusa RC for about two weeks, and el-Zaim and I made plans to escape. We took a walk and checked out the fence and spotted one of the Italian guards walking on the outside, so we called to him in Arabic and he lit our cigarettes. He told us he'd lived in Alexandria for three years and explained that there was no point in escaping: If you want to make a break for it, do it in Sicily. Lampedusa's a small island and there's nobody here but Italians. Everyone here's Italian and they're all police or army or border guards, because it's the closest island to the Arabs. Bottom line, it's a military zone with a small airport and the rest is a camp. More important, it's in the middle of the sea and it's a long way from here to Sicily, the nearest land.

One morning they called our names and moved us by plane to Sicily, where the RC's main headquarters are and where we'd decided to escape and get on the train to Milan. Muhammad el-Zaim and I had agreed to run the moment we arrived, before we had our fingerprints taken and were photographed, because if they catch you in Italy and they have your photograph, they'll know where you're coming from and they'll send you back to the Red Cross, and from there straight back to your country.

We got off the plane in a large place with a fence round it in the middle of the forest. There were people of every nationality you could think of. They put us in threes into a cell consisting of a portable room with three beds and a toilet, and told us, Tomorrow and the day after you're going to be photographed and fingerprinted and questioned. We'd boarded the plane in the afternoon and arrived before sunset and then had lunch, and we tried to get out of having our fingerprints taken but they took us and sent us in to see a Tunisian woman, Leila, who asked me for my name and nationality. I answered in Bedouin dialect and said, My name is Azam Abdallah Sfeit, from Iraq, and my dad and my mum and my brothers were killed in the war and I don't know where my sister is. I had an old razor scar on my belly so I showed it to her and said it was a war wound. She looked at it without the slightest sympathy and told me, I know you're not from Iraq and that your family weren't killed in the war and that you're a Mashrigi Bedouin from Egypt but I'm going to pass you anyway. She wrote down I was Iraqi and passed me. After I left her, I ran into a friend of mine from Nigeria who'd been with me in storage in Libya. He greeted me warmly and I told him, I want to make a break for it now. It was just my good luck that he was in that business. He took fifty euro per head. He told me, After sunset, and after you escape and jump over the fence, follow the high-tension pylons till they divide, left and right. Follow the right and don't leave it and it'll take you to the train that goes to Milan.

I went to the bathroom to wash the fingerprint ink off my hands and ran into el-Zaim and told him, Come on, let's make a run for it right now, and we agreed I'd go and set fire to the cell on the other side to distract the guards and he'd go and give the money to the guy from Nigeria who was going to help us. Then, as soon as the smoke went up from the cell, they'd throw the mattress onto the wire and we'd jump onto it and escape. The moment I'd set fire to the cell and gone into the bathroom, the fire caught and I heard a ruckus over by the fence. I ran back and caught sight of Muhammad el-Zaim's back as he flipped over from the mattress to the other side. I ran, calling out to him, Zaim! Zaim! and as I ran I heard the cell crackling. I got to the Nigerian, who was next to the fence, and used him to get a leg up. The fence was four meters high and it was topped with barbed wire and the mattress was on top of that. I climbed up and threw myself onto the mattress on my stomach and rolled over and fell down on the outside, landing on my feet in an irrigated field of corn, and the siren went off. I kept on running, calling, Zaim! Zaim! but el-Zaim had disappeared.

Moonshine

I WAS DEEP INTO RESEARCHING and reviewing the material for this book, when I got news of Bu Abdallah, my comrade-in-work-and-struggle in Libya. I heard it by accident from Said Jerjaresh back home. They'd found him strangled, arms tied behind his back, at his farm at Umm el-Araneb, south of Sabha. Frankly, it gave me a scare. I got goose-bumps and I sweated so much the guy didn't know what was going on. A terrifying movie reel of all the nights the two of us could have gotten killed, same way, same place, ran before my eyes. Umm el-Araneb was where we used to make moonshine, smuggle it into Sabha, and sell it by the liter at the cement-block factory.

Did I say "we"?

Actually, it was just Bu Abdallah who did the selling. I, being a dumbass, sold nothing. I took all the risk—made the alcohol, smuggled it, bagged it, and handed it over to the clients—but I refused to sell it, all because of a rigid, unbending creed.

Alcohol was banned in Libya, more than drugs. The punishment was life in prison, even death, but the authorities turned a blind eye to moonshine. They didn't make it legal, they just ignored it, and didn't do anything to the people who sold it unless they had a complaint from a citizen, which in fact was how they dealt with all criminals (though if the criminal was from the Leader's clan, you could bang your head on the wall for all the good it would do).

The moonshine I'm talking about is a down-and-dirty local drink. They used to say it was the one and only industrial product 100 percent locally produced in the Great State of the Masses. It's made of sugar and yeast and has a massive kick. A 50-kilo sack of sugar plus 50 kilos of yeast to a 100-liter barrel yields between sixty and seventy *leetras*, and one *leetra* will bring an elephant to its knees. My friend Muhammad el-Hutmani was a teacher who was so scared of the police and security services he shriveled up and died every time he saw a Saad-Shin soldier, but on one *leetra* of moonshine he'd turn into an ogre with a single idea in its head—vengeance on the police. He'd shout, "Screw the police! Swear to God I'm going to fuck the police!" till he had a fit and passed out. Once, when he was totally wasted, he rammed the police station itself with a car.

Bu Abdallah was regarded as the best moonshine-maker in Sabha, so, seeing I was his partner and hung out with him all the time, I used to help him, and seeing Bu Abdallah was an old guy of sixty and I was young and healthy and twenty, I ended up taking care of the whole operation.

At the beginning, I took delivery of lots, ready and bottled in jerry-cans, every Thursday, from Anwar el-Rumhi in Tayyouri Quarter. Usually it was three twenty-liter cans. Anwar was originally a Rumhi Bedouin from the Fayoum— bald, fat, cautious, and very timid. He'd gotten Saad-Shin status in the seventies and was officially a soldier in the Libyan army. Each time, he'd come up with a delivery method that would let him off the hook completely and make me the fall guy if the police came down on us. One time, he'd leave the cans out on the street and stand at a distance gazing at the sky as though he didn't know me. Another, he'd arrange them in front of his apartment, close the door as per normal, and make out like he was somebody else and in fact hated the whole business and had nothing whatever to do with it. In the end, he decided he was okay with passing them to me through the window and he'd hand them out to me in a steady stream from his apartment on the fourth floor and not give a hoot for the astonishment of the neighbors or passersby who saw him, while I caught them and hid them away, shaking with fear, not just of the police but of the people, who used to gather round and watch, totally bemused.

I was much relieved when Bu Abdallah got fed up with Anwar's fearful and disorganized approach to delivering the lot at the required time and decided to make it himself at the farm at Umm el-Araneb, which wasn't far from where he was. Its official owner, Jerjaresh, and the real owner, Muhammad Khuweiter, were customers of his and kept him going with hashish, moonshine, and even women if he wanted, which he usually did, and he'd work till morning. Then, every night, they'd drink, and sometimes they'd . . . (well, never mind about that) at his place in the factory's living quarters, and at the end of the night they'd make an armed attack on one of the other farms that were making moonshine and seize two or three jerry-cans to make up for the ones they'd drunk at Bu Abdallah's. Bu Abdallah had begun his career in moonshine by doing the distillation and only started working in sales after he joined us as a partner in the cement-block factory. He'd drop by and pick me up every Wednesday in a dark-blue Peugeot mini-truck with sacks of sugar and yeast, plus food and drink for two days and we'd get out at the Umm el-Araneb farm.

The farm consisted of thirteen hectares surrounded by a wall with two cement rooms and a bathroom, one room for sleeping in and another for making the moonshine. As soon as we arrived, we'd eat a bite and set about work, with all the seriousness, zeal, and contented buzz to be expected of men making moonshine in a country where it was banned. We'd clean the barrel well, till it shone, set it up over a large brazier, and fill it to the halfway point with water. Then we'd empty into it a 50-kilo sack of sugar and ten pounds' worth of yeast and he'd stir the solution with a ladle made out of a small shovel, adding water, and when the sugar and yeast had dissolved and the solution had begun to boil, he'd cover the barrel tightly with a plastic cover from which extended a pipe that went into a spigot at the bottom. From there the concentrated steam would drip into the jerry-can drop by drop.

Distilling a large barrel, which gave from three to four twenty-*leetra* jerry-cans, over low heat, could take from half a day to a whole day, and as soon as the operation was finished, we'd load the jerry-cans quickly into the truck and make a dash for Sabha. Or not a dash, but a very slow crawl. I'd drive the truck with Bu Abdallah next to me wearing a red tarbush, "like any Libyan," as camouflage, and with the jerry-cans exposed and jostling in the back, like jerry-cans of water (though in fact the moonshine was white). In addition, it became clear that this was the only method used by Libyan smugglers precisely because they weren't really smugglers by nature, just Bedouin bent on plunder. The dumbest thing, though, was that the red tarbush with the dangling black tassel, the tarbush that my uncle the headman used to wear when he gave the sermon at the eid, hadn't been worn by the Libyans themselves for ages, only by Egyptian Bedouin, especially those who worked in this kind of business. All the same, we'd pass safely through the three police checkpoints, with their bristling weapons, and make it to the cement-block factory and hide the cans quickly in the bathroom. Then Bu Abdallah and I would sit in the living quarters waiting for the clients.

Once, Khuweiter, "the Juhsi who kidnapped the wife of the Yugoslavian doctor," was with us and we were in his armored Toyota Landcruiser. When he saw the red security barrels blocking the entrance to Sabha, he said haughtily, "They're just piss pants, and they think they're police?" and he stepped on the gas, swerved into the other lane, and drove against the traffic with all the confidence and arrogance in the world, right before their eyes.

In fact, the factory's living quarters looked exactly right, for a hermit's cell, or for a bar in a barren land—a single room set on the summit of a small red mound. It was quickly turned, though, or Bu Abdallah quickly turned it, for purposes of camouflage, into the Mecca of every poor Egyptian Bedouin who'd come from our home district of Etsa, in the Fayoum, to work in Libya. Every single day, people came, people went, and people stayed overnight, spread around all over, indoors and out.

By day, the living quarters were just that—the living quarters of a factory for making cement blocks, and me and the guys working with me making the blocks spent our time between the shed and the blocks that were scattered in front of it, and if (I say, if) a customer for blocks came, we'd agree on a price for them. And by night, it was Bu Abdallah's business.

Forget the tragedy I suffered personally at his hands, Bu Abdallah was a larger-than-life character. Illiterate, from Bani Sueif, but larger-than-life all the same. He'd had thirteen passports forged in the names of his children and relatives in Egypt on the basis that they were "returnees" to Libya. For each of them he cashed the annual stipend that the Leader allocated to his people and his fellow citizens, which Bu Abdallah just went on collecting and sending off to Egypt.

Bu Abdallah was also brown and bald, with a thick mustache that gave the impression of flapping to and fro as he spoke. A Rumhi Saad-Shin from Bani Sueif. His business began distribution in the afternoon and continued till after sundown—a *leetra* poured into a plastic bag from the jerry-can in the bathroom and handed over to the customers who came by the quarters. Most of them were Libyan youths who'd stolen something to pay for their *leetra* of moonshine. At night, it was a hashish den. Hashish for the ones who were into hashish, alcohol for the ones who were into alcohol, and for those who were into both there were both. And there was I, not drinking because of stuff to do with my beliefs and Bu Abdallah not drinking because of stuff to do with work. Sometimes he'd be obliged to bring Ghanaian women to the workshop and wait for them to finish to get his money and sometimes he'd bring one back to the quarters. On such occasions his mustache really flapped, and he'd sleep like a corpse for two days.

The Forest

I RAN ALONE THROUGH THE corn and after the corn the forest, and the moment I got into the forest a helicopter came, with a spotlight that turned it into daylight, and it passed right over me, but I kept on running. I ran for about three hours with that helicopter right over me—God knows how they did it—then found a rock and hid till it went away, and I came out and walked, following the high-tension pylons, like the Nigerian had told me to.

A forest like I used to see in the movies. Esparto grass up to my chest, trees that closed above my head, and all the sounds you hear in a forest. I was walking next to the high-tension line and every now and then I'd be startled, like get the shock of my life, by quail suddenly going *firrrrr!* from right under my feet. It was dark, not much moonlight, and at about one I came across an ordinary-looking oblong of short grass I thought was a regular path. I took a couple of steps and began sinking. Another step and I was being swallowed. That moment I saw my whole life—my life and my death—and I thought I was going to die right there: You're going to die and no one will know anything about what happened to you—not your family, not Italy, not anybody. I twisted around with all my strength, kicked back against the grass and kept grabbing at it till its sharp ends hit me in my face and chest and made me bleed. I screamed, *Aaaargh*! and after a while felt an embankment or a wall or whatever made of concrete and heaved myself up onto it. I tried to draw breath but couldn't. Dawn had begun to break. I looked around and saw that the hellhole that had almost done me in was a long ditch hidden under esparto grass. I stood up and walked along the concrete for about a kilometer till I came to a little bridge. I crossed it, returned to the pylons, and kept going till they forked, left and right. I took the right. The sun was up. I came across some barbed wire with chickens, kids, and donkeys inside, and a field planted with watermelons and honeydews. I was dying of hunger and thirst and fell on the melons and ate till I felt my belly was going to explode, like a rotten egg. Then I raised my eyes and saw a house, a small villa in the middle of the farm with washing hung out to dry. My clothes were all covered with mud and I walked toward it so as to take something to wear but when I got to it I found two black dogs, each as big as a lion, that barked with a terrifying sound and leaped at me. I backed off in a hurry and tried to jump the wire. My pants got caught so I rolled over onto the other side but my pants got ripped and my thigh along with them and I kept on going.

At seven or eight o'clock, I came upon train tracks and thought, This must be the train that goes to Milan, and followed them. They ran on an elevated trestle with the forest spread out beneath. A little further on I came across a dirt track leading to an army camp—a gate with soldiers and two armored cars in front and the Italian flag flying overhead. I was tired, I had no strength left, and I was dying of thirst. I would have handed myself over to the devil himself so I went down to them. There were four soldiers and an officer, who was sitting on a chair. I was pretty much a walking lump of mud and blood. I said to the officer in Egyptian, I'm Egyptian. Take me! Take me anywhere! He said, *Vaaa!* I knelt at his feet, acted out my plight, waved my arms about, jumped up and down, and still it was *Vaaa!*, and he gestured to the soldiers and they dragged me by my pants back to the road. As I got up, I caught sight of another, big, road in the middle of the forest with eight lanes and cars flashing by and on either side I saw water bottles that had been thrown away and still had some water in them. I threw myself on them and drank about seven. Then I got up and waved to the cars. One would come along—*vroom*—and not stop and another—*vroom*—and not stop and another —*vroom*—and not stop till *vroom*, one stopped a little further on and flashed its lights and backed up and a dark-skinned guy got out and asked me in Arabic, Are you on the run from the RC? and before I could reply, he said, Come on, and he opened the door and got in and moved over and I got in next to him in the back. I saw two blond girls next to him, and the driver was Italian and there was another woman next to him. The man kept asking me questions and I kept answering them till we got to the apartment building where he was living. We got out and climbed to the third floor. It turned out he was Sudanese and had come here a long time ago and had Italian nationality. To my good fortune he was my height exactly and he gave me jeans, a T-shirt, a jacket, and shoes and socks of his, and I had a shower and felt fine. He told me, Listen, I'll get you a ticket to Milan and put you on the plane, but first you have to get a relative or friend of yours over there to transfer me five hundred euros. I told him, I'm sorry I don't have anyone and I don't know anyone. He said, How come, man? That won't do! Never mind, I told him. Just thanks for the clothes and the shower and everything. We're all Arabs and brothers and you'll be well rewarded in Heaven. Now, if you don't mind, just take me to the station for Milan.

The Smugglers' Song

THIS IS A SONG ABOUT smuggling from Egypt to Libya dating to either before or during the time of the Leader, I don't remember exactly. Anyway, if every story has its song, this is the song of the Saad-Shin:

Lady of the luscious locks, I greet you!
                                        Listen to my well-ordered verses!
The verses I speak are of people who smuggle,
                    Two-thirds of them poor men with empty purses.
Two-thirds of them, I say, poor folk
                                        just putting on a smuggler's airs,
Forever caught up, poor sods, in the dream
                            even when spending the night behind bars!
And I, fair lady, was just such a one,
                                        just sixty pounds to my name—
At a loss what goods I could buy
                                so to the produce-sellers I came.
To the Salloum market we came,
                            to Bu Wafi, whose goods are first-rate.
We bought from him zucchini and garlic
                                and loaded two gross, give or take.
I said to the stall's owner,
                            God preserve your earnings and bless ye!
But Bu Wafi just counted his money—
                                he'd gotten, of my sixty, fifty-three.

We loaded, my sister, some donkeys
                    and how often we've carried more than we ought!
Let come what may! said we,

                              and set off for the gap at the fort,
And through that same gap we crossed back—
                              · not an officer in sight, not a black.
We felt sure we were going to make it
                              but a checkpoint hove into sight—
I told him, Mister, we've already crossed over.

                              Please, don't make me eat shite!
Befriend me, be my partner—
                    we're from here and homewards making our way.
He said, Bribes, we don't take them.

                    We don't need them, we're doing okay.
The goods we'll send over
                    then the guys in the office can do as they please.
I say, Hear me out, Sergeant,
                    God be kind to your parents and to you too grant ease!
Do me a favor, don't put on an act!

                    Most of you guys are bent, that's a known fact.
Get moving, you bum! he shouts.

                              Don't pull that stuff on me!
God willing, a year you'll rot here
                              and the goods you'll never see.
I say, Look me in the eye and make certain—
                              I saw you at Rocky Path.
Think you can deny it? You know you can't—
                              You took me for a pound and a half!
Says he, Swear to God I've never seen you!
                    This is the first time we've met in our lives
But we're going to bring ruin down upon you—
                    We're not the type that takes bribes!
When I saw the high horse he was riding,
                    so I saluted and gave him a smoke.

I thought, Maybe he'll change his tune now

               and give us a break, us poor folk.

How long, sister, we pleaded!

             But he had us, so it didn't matter how hard,

And off to the fort he took us,

              us walking ahead under guard

In pitiful state, like all the Bedouin that came before us!

          And they took us, my brothers, to the fort.

Then along came Bu Erfan and he saw us.

         He asked them, By whom were these brought?

They said, We're the ones who brought them

          but it's you must decide what's to come.

Help them, for the sake of their children!

         They don't look like they mean any harm.

No way, said he, will I help them!

         Fetch me my whip and I'll flog them!

You, Muhammad, take down their names.

         Tell me who's this and who's that.

So the man sets down our names in writing—

         an evil-eyed scowling black—

And reads us questions out loud,

      saying, You all, where are you when you stay put?

I tell him, Mister, I'm doing okay,

         I'm an Azmi from Kingi Maryout

Where the people who come visit are well-heeled

         while we live a life with no rest.

He said, You mean you're from el-Amriya?

         I told him, A little bit more to the west.

Then he gives me a sidelong glance,

         asks, Where have I seen you before?

I say, Wherever we have pastures you'll find me—

         everyone in the world here knows me

But you all have treated me bad—

         you're always giving me hell.

Come with me right now, the man said,

                         and to Bu Erfan tell your tale.

This work's no crime

                         so why are you scared?

They took me to Abd el-Hamid—

          he turned out harsher, just when I thought we'd be spared.

He said, Put irons on his wrist

                      and write their names twice in a list.

I tell him, O Abd el-Hamid,

                  O Bu Erfan, God increase your seed,

Listen to my words and look me in the eye

                       I do this stuff so my kids won't die.

He asked me, Haven't you heard the news

                  that's on the radio day in day out?

We're fighting the infidels,

                 and you're taking rations out?

To our east on the borders

                  we're out fighting the Jews

(May God of His bounty bring them no closer!).

               How come you don't read the news?

I tell him, sir, I'm no scholar.

               I can't read or write my name—

Which is Jweida Bu el-Hawal,

               poet, of wide-spread fame.

Ask Bu Zawwam about me—

               a man all politesse and proper ways,

A sound man who condones no wrongdoing

          but for loosing men's shackles e'er wins praise—

You with a sash round your waist like a Bedouin of yore!

          And You, by Your majesty, O Forgiving Lord—

Relieve us of this trade, which has brought us to the gates of Hell—

A man well-known am I, raised among princes, and raised well!

The Train

I SPENT THE NIGHT AT the Sudanese guy's place and at five in the morning he put me behind him on his Vespa and took me to the station. My plan was to get on the train and keep out of sight of the ticket collector any way I could, but when I went inside and onto the platform, I found more than forty Egyptians on the run from the RC like me and just as they were, with the dirt and mud they'd brought with them from the forest. And not only that, but they were sitting huddled together as though they'd already been rounded up and were under arrest, and all of them looking in the direction the train would come from. I went over to them and said, I'm Egyptian like you, and the way you're sitting will bring the police down on us at any moment, and I was just telling them, You have to split up and not stick together in groups, when I saw someone poke his head round the station master's door, look at us, then go in again. I told them, That guy's going to get the police, and I left them and walked toward the far end of the station. I put my head over the wall and saw two truckloads of police going into the station. I thought of going back and warning them but I was scared so I walked normally for about four steps, then jumped over the wall and out of the station.

I ran down the street till I came to a ditch like the one I'd almost died in in the forest, about four meters wide and three deep with a little water in the middle, the four meters being silt with thick cane not less than three meters high growing out of it. I stepped into the middle of the cane, parting it and fixing it to make a place where I could stay till the police, who had actually arrested the other Egyptians and begun putting them into trucks, had gone away. Next to where I was in the reeds, I could hear people bargaining—No, five hundred's too much! No, only three hundred!—so I pushed through the reeds and made my way toward the voice. Who's there?—Who's there? it said. Egyptian! Egyptian! I said, and suddenly I came upon them and found two young kids from el-Menoufiya and with them two kids from Sudan. They were arguing over the price of a ticket to Milan. The Sudanese were saying five hundred, the Egyptians only three. I saw the opportunity at once so I got involved and took the Egyptians aside and talked them into paying five hundred each and I took the Sudanese aside and talked them into taking a thousand for three. We agreed and they went to get us food and we spent the night in the ditch. At five the Sudanese came back again and took the thousand euro and brought us the tickets and we went into the station. I noticed a Moroccan-looking guy putting Muhammad el-Zaim into the second car on the train. We got onto the train. The ticket collector came: Where are your tickets? and he started muttering and mewing and fuming and his face turned even redder than it already was and we didn't understand anything till the Moroccan who'd put el-Zaim onto the train came along: Your tickets aren't for this train. This is the Milan train that only stops once in each province, at the big cities. It goes from Sicily starting with Palermo, then Tatania, then Naples, then Rome, then Milan, and these tickets of yours cost precisely one euro and take you one stop inside Sicily and not on this train either.

Of course, the Sudanese weren't there: they'd melted into thin air at the station. The thousand euros were gone, the train had left, and we all sat down, flat broke.

We got to know the Moroccan who'd put el-Zaim on the train. He listened to our plight and it turned out he was a smuggler too. He took us to his apartment, where I found el-Zaim's relations, who'd left me while I was setting fire to the cell and escaped from the RC along with him. They said el-Zaim had gone to Milan so he could send 1500 euros to the Moroccan so he could put them on the train too. They were staying with the Moroccan as a guarantee till he sent the money and they'd phoned el-Zaim and el-Zaim hadn't answered. I told them, He won't answer and he won't give a damn. I'm his friend and I know him well.

The two kids from el-Menoufiya who were with me phoned their relatives in Milan and they sent the Moroccan a thousand euros, not to put them on the train but to keep them at his place till their fancy private car could arrive, which it did, and took them. After a while, the family of the two kids from el-Sarira, el-Zaim's relatives, sent them a thousand euros and I was the only one left without money or contacts. The Moroccan said to me, And what about you? so I told him, I've got nothing. Thanks for the food and the hospitality but you can take me back to the station the way you brought me.

The Desert Nightingale

THE SINGER WAS, BY ORIGIN, a Malki Bedouin from el-Am-riya near Alexandria. He'd gone to Libya "under the wire" as a boy of fifteen, and in Libya they immediately accepted him as a Malki. He obtained a Saad-Shin ID card and went to work for a construction company. One day, a State Security officer came and asked for the names of all the Saad-Shin workers. There were about forty of them in addition to the Singer, the Bedouin praise-sayer and master of nuptial ceremonies Bu Gargour, and Saleh Bu Habbouna. The following day, they rounded them up, put them in trucks, and sent them off to the army. The Singer, however, fled. In those days, the only singing he'd done was at parties held by his workmates, where they played the Bedouin lyre. He returned to Egypt to begin his career as a singer, everything changed, and he became the celebrated Awad Bu Abd el-Gader el-Malki, the most famous Bedouin singer in Egypt and Libya. One day, or rather night, he was killed in an incident on his way home from a celebration in honor of the 1st of September Revolution that had been attended by the Leader himself. Some say it was an accident, others that it was a set-up. A trailer truck crushed him as he was driving back to Egypt at dawn in the Mercedes Benz the Leader had presented to him. At the celebration, he'd played, for the Leader and for the 1st of September, his famous song about Libya:

You are Great, and as such he named you,
You are Great, through the Green Book
And Muammar,
Your army and your defiant people!
When the Cowboy strikes he seeks to destroy you
But God's help is ever with you.
You are Great, and as such he named you.

Awad el-Malki was a thirty-five-year-old Bedouin singer who wrote his own lyrics and tunes. He had a voice like thunder. He was distinguished by his good looks, his sartorial elegance, and his overwhelming courtesy, and was greatly loved by the young Bedouin of both Egypt and Libya. We thought of him as the Abd el-Halim Hafez of the desert. I and all my generation would "ride our camels" as though to some holy mosque in order to attend his parties, whether in the neighborhood or anywhere else in the Fayoum. They used to put up a stage made of five or six trailers in the middle of the desert and people would come in their thousands, bringing with them the cassette recorders from Iraq that were the rage then.

El-Malki was born in Alexandria, in el-Maamoura:

Walking on the shore at el-Maamoura
I was met by a cute young signora
I matched my steps to hers
And forgot I was Bu Gaddoura

as one of his songs goes. He played the *majruna* and sang all the different kinds of Bedouin song—the *shteiwa*, the *alam*, the *ghinnawa* and the *gol el-ajwad*, excelling particularly at the *alam*. It seems, though, that his words and tunes went unnoticed in the barren desert so he returned to his home ground and became the star singer at Bedouin weddings from Alexandria to Aswan and issued dozens of tapes. His strong, flexible voice rang out in every dialect and to every rhythm, and he formed a professional Bedouin band and became well-known. He developed Bedouin song and made it more diverse, with new tunes and instruments such as the lute and the violin, never before used in the history of western Bedouin song in Egypt. He made his recordings in the Fayoum, Egypt's center of Bedouin song production in the days of the cassette recorder, and issued dozens of tapes, which found a wide audience among the young people of the Bedouin tribes of both Egypt and Libya. He became arguably their favorite singer in the popular style, or at least a favored singer and permanent fixture at celebrations commemorating the 1st of September Revolution of Libya's Great State of the Masses.

That particular year, Awad el-Malki had come to Libya to attend two events—the 1st of September holiday and Gaddafi's demolition, for the first time in history, of the gates at the Egypt-Libya border. (The Leader got on the bulldozer himself and destroyed the gates, chanting, "Down with Colonialist Borders that Shackle Mankind!") At about the same time, American planes bombed and rocketed Gaddafi's own house. During those days, a rumor went around among our Libyan brothers, including a number of my friends who were in the know, that Gaddafi was in high good humor because he thought that a divine veil had wrapped itself around him and protected him from the American bombs, and Awad el-Malki sang, for him and for all of Libya:

> *First, on the Great Masses' name I call—*
> > *before the world it said, No more!*
> *Second, on Libya's own name I call—*
> > *above all men your glories soar!*
> *Third, on your people's socialism I call—*
> > *humiliation they abhor!*

At night, gossip circulated to the effect that Awad had been drinking with his friends during the celebration and may have drunkenly made fun of the person of the Leader himself. Anyway, on the morning of 15 September 1991, he was crushed to death beneath a trailer truck.

Milan

IN THE MORNING, THE MOROCCAN took us to the station and bought the Sarira kids tickets while I stared at the train, looking for a place I could stow away. He gave me a ticket, though, saying, It costs one hundred and sixty euro. If you want to pay me back, do so; if you don't, God will, and may He forgive you. I almost choked with joy and told him, Don't worry. I swear to God I'll pay you back. I hugged him, tears running down my cheeks, and got on the train.

So the three of us set off. We sat there, waiting throughout the journey for the loudspeaker to announce, Milano! We arrived at eleven at night and acted the way we'd been told. We left the station in a perfectly normal way, joking and laughing with one another, like we were natives of the country coming home after a trip. Inside, though, I was terrified and felt like the whole station was staring at us. We found their relatives waiting for them and they took us on the subway to their apartment in Loreto, and I freshened up, washed my clothes, and went to sleep. At seven in the morning, they all went off to work and just the two who'd come with me were left. After we'd had breakfast, they hinted gently that it wouldn't do for me to stay.

I went down to the street. My first street in a country that wasn't mine and a world that wasn't mine, and I felt myself growing larger with the cleanness, the neatness, and the good air. The street was paved with stone, like a wall but built on the ground, and very smooth, and it shone in the sun. I walked till I found a public telephone office with Arabic writing on the outside. I went in and found an Egyptian from el-Menoufiya and I told him, I'm on the run from the RC and I don't have any money and I want to call my family in Egypt. He said, Go ahead. I called our house in Egypt and got the number of Mahmoud Bu el-Fadl, my friend who'd left for Italy two years before, and I called him. It turned out he was working on the scaffolded apartment building right in front of me across from the telephone office.

Bu el-Fadl put me behind him on his Vespa and we went to his home outside Milan in a place called Baranzate, at the end of the No.12 subway. The apartment was rented by his brother, Hasan, and a friend of his from el-Gharg—a bedroom, living room, corridor, kitchen, and bathroom. There were three bunk beds, one of which was unoccupied because the person who'd been sleeping in it had gone back to Egypt. I slept in it for two days and they made me pay rent. My family paid it to the Egyptian owner of the apartment over there.

I spent a month with Bu el-Fadl and it was then that I saw the Italy I'd always heard about, "the Italy of your dreams," as they say—work, drink, girls, and freedom. We worked as plasterers during the week and on Saturday nights we'd go to a place called Parco Sempione, or "the Castello," a *huuuge* garden, with a castle from Roman times that looked like the Citadel of Qaitbey, only smaller, and had a gate with statues on top of it. Every Saturday they held a party there—a really, really big party—with dancing, singing, and drinking till morning. Sometimes we'd even sleep there and wake in the morning to find police dogs sniffing at us. Then we'd get on the Vespa and go back to the apartment in Baranzate, rest for two or three hours, and at night go back in to a place called the Domo, which is in the middle of the city and has a statue of the Virgin Mary made of solid gold. The church is surrounded by old buildings and in front there's a large open space paved with marble, a statue of a knight on horseback at the entrance, and next to it a broad stairway that goes up to a wide terrace that looks out over the open space and where people drink and party. Mahmoud and I used to sit there and drink, and young people would come and drink with us, boys and girls, and we'd dance and sing and go wild. If one person fancied another, they'd do whatever they wanted with complete freedom. Once a group of guys with long hair came, each with his girlfriend and his dog, bringing a bag holding twenty bottles of red wine. We got down to it and drank the twenty bottles. They took off with their dogs around four in the morning, leaving us so drunk we couldn't get down again or even speak. There are about twenty marble steps, which we tumbled down head over heels till we landed all over the place at the bottom. We were supposed to get subway No.12, which would take us to Barazante but there was a bar next to the subway station with a little garden where we sat and had a hell of a good time. We came to at noon to the yelling of the owner of the bar about Arabs who couldn't find anywhere to sleep. We went on like that for a month. The days when we didn't have work we'd get drunk and be rowdy till morning. The next month, work stopped and the man whose bed I'd been sleeping in came back from Egypt and things started going bad for me. I found out about the churches and eating in the churches and I met people from everywhere. Long lines for every meal. At first I was ashamed of myself and then I got used to it.

As el-Mutanabbi says,

He who humiliates himself is easily humiliated.
A wound causes a dead man no pain.

Kidnapping, Day In Day Out

KIDNAPPINGS, MUGGINGS, AND SHAKE-DOWNS were common in Sabha. Two or three kids would run into you and clean you out, and the people who most often got mugged, or, rather, the ones least likely to offer resistance, were the Egyptians. Worse, most of these kids were from the Industrial Quarter. They'd wait for Egyptians at the way in at night and then it would be like, "Empty your pockets, pissy little Egyptian!" and the Egyptian would empty his pockets. If it was an Algerian, or even a Sudanese, he'd object, maybe even fight, but not an Egyptian. I was always quarrelling with el-Hasnawi, Abd el-Aziz, and Rashid the Tunisian, the guy who'd driven the boat, about this. I kept telling them, "The civilized man is always fearful. I'm telling you a truth about the human experience: fear is part and parcel of the progress of nations." El-Hasnawi would shrug and say, "And I'm telling you that Egyptians are, and I'm sorry to say this, cowards by nature. Absolutely, for no particular reason, and about everything."

Whatever. Let's stick to muggings in Sabha. I, personally, was mugged a lot. Once, when we were at the factory's living quarters in Tayyouri Quarter, four Libyan kids with pistols attacked. One said, "Where's the money?" There were four workers with me, two of them my cousins and two from the Rubeiat tribe, from Giza. One was terrified and when one of the kids asked him, "Where's the money, piss pants?" he pointed to me, saying, "It's with Hamdi." The kid came toward me and pressed the pistol to my cheek, pushing the muzzle up against the bone and screaming, "Hand over the money!"

I fear violence. I'm terrified by any thug, even if it's a small child. But I'm not afraid of guns. Or perhaps I get seized by some blank state conducive to a kind of dumb courage. I also firmly believe that only cowards resort to guns. In my opinion, a genuinely brave guy doesn't carry a gun—in fact, he's dead scared of carrying guns. Anyway, I believe that the person who thought up the idea of guns was a coward to begin with. He didn't know what to do about people who scared him so he thought up guns. If he'd been capable of defending himself on his own, he'd never have thought up gunpowder, bombs, and guns. Mankind will never advance and never be truly at ease anywhere until it disarms.

I don't know where I got the idea that the revolver the Libyan kid was carrying and that was pressed against my cheek was a toy, but I said, with total confidence and self-assuredness, "Get that toy out of my face, kid!"

This response brought the game to an end, and the kid put away his pistol and said, "What's wrong with you, man? We were just messing with you!"

Every day we heard news of kidnappings and muggings of Egyptians, Sudanese, and Africans, but the police and the government in Sabha did nothing. A rumor went round that they were in cahoots with the perpetrators, or the kidnappers were in fact from their ranks. The Sabha police weren't really any different, even in terms of appearance and the clothes they wore, from kidnappers.

Kidnapping was so normal in Sabha that even the wife of a Yugoslavian doctor working there was kidnapped, and everything was turned upside down while they looked for her. The Yugoslavian regime, being socialist, was on good terms with the Leader's, and the Yugoslavian ambassador made an official protest.

In the end, though, it was nothing to do with the ambassador and the Yugoslavian revolution. In essence, it's just a custom we have, both as institutions and individuals. Think of it as an exaggerated expression of our hospitality toward foreigners, and even, I might say, toward enemies. We care more about the plight of others than we do about our own, even though we usually attribute ours to them, whether in Egypt or Iraq, or even Tunisia. The over-concern for the calamity-befallen foreign national (and even more so, dear God, if it's some poor Egyptian or African who's come here to work) and the indifference to or even sometimes physical abuse of the local national is, I feel, a widely shared Arab habit that one might call "the obsession with the foreigner" and the Western foreigner especially—calling him an infidel, despising him, and at the same time being obsessed with and panicked by him. After all, as I don't need to tell you, an Arab can only obsess over something if he simultaneously declares it forbidden fruit.

So the Leader himself came to Sabha and stood up and said, "I gonna fix this meself!" and I personally saw him fix it 'imself. He stopped cars himself and examined their papers, and if he found anything wrong with them it was like, "On your knees, piss pants!" and he let loose into the streets and squares a well-equipped army of Saad-Shin, who fixed Sabha and had it working like clockwork in no time.

The Hamlet

THE PLACE WE CALLED THE Hamlet was in Porta Genova, on the edge of the forest. When you leave the forest, you'll find two streets. The street on the right leads to the last stop for bus 90/91, the one they call "the Bullock" because it goes round and round the city and runs twenty-four hours.

If you go past the front of the Hamlet, you'll find the *naviglio*, a canal dug to boost tourism, which has coffee shops on both sides. Cross the big bridge that goes over it, walk a little, and you'll find yourself in the Domo, where we used to party at night, and then at the stop for streetcars 7, 9, and 14. Continue in the same direction on foot and you'll find yourself at the Domo church. Leave that at your back and you'll find yourself in the Porta Genova market, the thieves' market, an ordinary weekly market that's got a stolen-goods section. Go in and you'll find stolen stuff, from bicycles, broad-screen TVs, and computers to cell phones, cigarette lighters, and underpants, spread out over the stands and even the ground. It's all Arabs, and as soon as the police turn up, they grab their stuff and disappear, and when the police have gone again, they come back.

The Hamlet consists of an old government building that begins with a narrow passageway between two walls. Then, when you go in and turn left, you find a big arch with a whole floor on top of it. Off this are two buildings, one tall, one low, or you could say it forms the head of a triangle of which the two buildings are two of the sides with the forest as the base.

The Hamlet is an old government building that was taken over by six Egyptian brothers. They were legal and had Italian papers. The oldest was a construction *capo* and he'd brought the others along to work with him on a job. Then one day they got their families and their workers' families together and took up residence in the old building and called it the Hamlet. When the government came, they refused to let them in, arguing they were Italian citizens and had nowhere else to go. Then they went into the wooded space between the two buildings, gathered stone from there and from the remains of buildings and apartment blocks throughout the neighborhood, and made it into a real proper hamlet. They built sixty rooms round it and rented them out. Each room held six and everyone paid a hundred euros a month. Some rooms were occupied by families and everyone was Egyptian, with sixty percent of them working in drugs, the rest thieves, burglars, beggars, and people who lived off the churches.

I moved in there with a bunch from el-Sharqiya to a room with three bunk beds, a broad-screen TV, a receiver, and electricity provided by a wire from the apartment building, and I stayed there about twenty days. I'd go out in the morning, have breakfast at the church, and wander through the streets, but the only work to be had was in construction, which meant one day on and ten off. I saw people bringing in hashish and one day I was late going to breakfast at the church and overslept, and when I woke up I found one of them sitting there and smoking a few joints. He gave me one and it got me high and I laughed a lot and then I cried. What's the matter? he said, and I said, I came here to be a millionaire—a millionaire, can you believe it!—and I can't even find the money for breakfast! He said, Why not work retail? I said, What do you mean retail? He reached his hand under the pillow on his bed and brought out a stick of hashish of the kind that goes for a hundred pounds in Egypt and he told me, Take this and go out to the entrance of the Hamlet and you'll find someone waiting there. Give it to him and then it's up to you. God willing you'll get him to pay a hundred euros and I'll take ten from you tomorrow morning. I stuck it into my pocket and went out and looked around. I found an Italian kid of about fifteen wearing his school uniform and while I was thinking, Who's that and what am I supposed to say to him? he asks me, Hashish? and the moment I brought out the stick he grabbed it and gave me fifty euros and left. I did the same again a second time, and a third, and a fourth, and then I took a *qirsh* and cut it into fingers and buried them in the forest. I began selling in the neighborhood of the Hamlet and four months later I got arrested. The police raided the Hamlet and arrested me with about twenty others. By luck, I didn't have anything on me. They took me inside: Name? Nationality? I was afraid they'd send me back, so I said, Azam Abdallah Sfeit, from Iraq, and I'm running away from the war. They kept me twelve hours in the lock-up, took my fingerprints, and let me go.

A Dawn Visit

WHEN YOU'RE MAKING CEMENT BLOCKS in a city as hot as Sabha, work begins at four in the morning and ends at eight a.m., or at the latest nine. It's so hot that if you work after that, you're committing suicide, literally. At first, I worked on my own. I was committed to fulfilling all the clauses of the contract, with Bu Abdallah putting in the money and me the effort. After a while, though, when it began to become clear that the factory was just a front for selling moonshine, I began to slack off and got two laborers from the marketplace to help me. I limited my own task to sprinkling the previous day's output of blocks with water, while the two hired hands did the work.

One day, or rather one night, after they'd woken up and pulled themselves together and I'd begun sprinkling the blocks and stirring the mixture and washing down the block-making machine . . .

(By the way, we had two machines in the factory. The second of which I'd made myself, or which the Lebanese guy had made under my supervision in his workshop right next to the factory. He was a very clean and handsome Lebanese man who was short, a little fat, with a plump red face and silvery-white hair that hung down at the back. If you saw him, you'd say he was an airline pilot, he was so smart and clean and well-mannered. His workshop was large, the profession required considerable skill, and his clients were numerous. He was in his sixties and worked alone, and every single night he'd have a different kind of African girl with him. He'd reassure me confidently, "Don't worry about your old dad. I put it in a glass of whiskey and that gets rid of any danger," and then he'd explode with laughter.

The gravel and sand were brought by a Mauritanian. I've forgotten his name. He was a light-skinned young man, thin and laconic, and I loved riding around with him and roaming the depths of the desert. He got the cement from an Egyptian contractor, the one who at the end gave me the money I used to run back to Egypt. The materials—the sand, cement, and gravel—were subsidized and they gave you a construction grant as well. Generally speaking, the Leader showered the Libyan people with stuff. Everything was subsidized, from gravel to cement to macaroni. And when I say showered, I mean showered: everything a person might need was totally subsidized.)

. . . and so, anyway, before dawn, just as the laborers had begun working, a pickup carrying four kids, two in front and two in back, burst in on us. The pickup came to a stop between the area and the two workmen, and the two in front got out, joined the ones in back, and they picked up a sheep's carcass, each taking a corner, and threw it to the ground. One of them screamed, "Pissy little thieves!" Then he came toward me and said, "You stole this from Shayeb's farm. We're taking you to the police right now."

I went up to him and said, in a voice I tried to make as Libyan and jokingly neutral and diffident as possible, "What's going on, man? What do you mean we stole it when you just turned up with it?"

"You stole it!" he screamed. "We're taking you to the police right now!" and he flung out his arm and whipped open a switchblade. In those days, security in Sabha was completely out of control, and Egyptians especially were getting shaken down almost on a daily basis—they'd even hand over whatever they had on them right off the bat, which was the safest thing to do, then negotiate till they could fob them off with whatever. But this wasn't a street mugging. It was the factory, the living quarters, the place where half the town slept! Plus the guys who did these things were dumb and would never give up when they thought they'd got you on the run, and the moment you gave in, they'd jump on top of you and beat you to a pulp and very possibly murder you and be pleased as Punch about it too. I was afraid, of course, but I felt a kind of hot flush mounting from below and running up me till it burst out of my eyes. I took two steps back and asked him, "Could you give me a minute?" My odd—or perhaps I should say ter-rified— question seemed to confuse him, because he turned to his companions and said, "What did he say?" which gave me a chance to take on board the nature of my plight and move closer to Atiya.

Atiya was a kid from the Rabayea Bedouin of Giza. I never saw him again but I'll never forget him. He was stir-ring, or pretending to stir, the cement mix. The guy came towards me, prodded me in the shoulder with the knife, and said, "You'd better do what I say!" and in the twinkling of an eye Atiya had pulled the spear-like shovel out of the mix and was whirling it over his and their heads, and they'd all thrown themselves onto the ground and begun crawling towards him, pleading with him like little children: "We're just messing with you, man! We stole it from Shayeb's farm for you to grill." So Atiya pulled out a knife and skinned it and we sat there grilling away together till morning.

The Squat

I GAVE UP THE HASHISH business. I was afraid they'd arrest and deport me. The rent built up month after month and the guy who rented the room threw me out, so el-Zaim took me to the basement of an apartment building where he slept in Famagosta. I spent that day and the next there. Then the owner of that building turned me out. I thought, There's nothing for it. In front of the building there was a small garden with a bridge over it. I got my stuff and brought a mattress and a blanket from the church to add to the blanket I had with me and set up a decent bed under the bridge and settled down there. Six a.m., I'd wash up and have breakfast at the Parco La Fatitsi, which we called Giardino Heweidi because a Bedouin from the Fayoum called Heweidi was always there. I'd walk through the streets, have lunch at the church at the Sisyo Centrale, Milan's main train station, and dinner at the Streetcar 14 church, which served lunch and dinner, though lunch at the Sisyo Centrale was better.

I stayed there three months and got to know every bit of Milan. I loved walking there however I was, with money or without, with a place or on the streets. It calmed me down— *vaaaaast*, vast, vast. It felt like a country and some people say it was one a long time ago. It has everything, and a human being, no matter how white or how black he is, or even if he's an infidel, can do whatever he likes there with complete freedom so long as he keeps himself to himself and doesn't harm anyone else.

People from the village and my Fayoum Bedouin relatives would pass me and not seem to know who I was. What was I? A *barbone*?—which means a beggar, or not just any beggar but a real piece of trash. And then, when things were going better for me and I had a house and was spending thousands, they came back to me, fawning like dogs.

It was under the bridge that I got to know the most decent and generous people I've ever met—a Christian family, who'd arrived there twenty years ago. First George came to see me. I'd been too lazy to go eat breakfast at the church and was sitting and stretching on my bed under the bridge. Where are you from? The Fayoum. Where are you from? Asyut. We smoked a joint together. The next day, he and his brother Michael came and he told me, We're inviting you to have lunch at home. I was too shy to go, but she turned up herself—George's mother, the mother who found me in a strange land and took it upon herself to make sure I ate and drank and had clothes to wear and who kept urging me to marry an Italian girl who could get me an official residence permit . . . though unfortunately things turned out very differently.

One day Rashid turned up and was like, Where are you living? I told him, Under the *bunta*. He said, Come and live with me at the squat in Famagosta. The squat consisted of an old building they'd cleared out for restoration. It had two apartments on each story, each fastened shut with an iron padlock and with a wide corridor between them, and Rashid and a relative of his were living there. It looked nice and sheltered. I'd been living in the street so I brought my bedding and moved in with them. A little later, el-Zaim had a quarrel with his relatives and came to live with us too.

Rashid was dealing drugs—hashish and cocaine. He asked, Do you want to work? There was nothing else to do so he gave us half a *qirsh* and we took it to where we were going to work—a large park with a children's garden and a dog area and if you went in a little, you found a large faucet that ran the whole time. We learned how and where to stash the goods there so if the police paid us a surprise visit, there'd be nothing to connect us to them. He gave us some advice: Don't leave the park. Walk around, sit down, it's up to you. Don't worry about the customers. They'll find you because of the way you look, like Arabs. No one else works in drugs around here except us. Even if you're not working in hashish, he'll say to you, *Fum?* and you say to him, *Fumo!* and you agree on the price. Get the money first, look around this way and that, pretend to bend down to look at something, grab the stuff you've stashed, and give it to him.

So we set to work. We'd cut a *qirsh* into sticks and sell it all in less than two hours. Things began to take off and the money was pouring in. I began wearing high-end labels and eating at the best restaurants, and the people who'd run away from me when I was living as a bum under the bridge came back and treated me with respect and stayed up late with me in bars. We began selling cocaine along with the hashish and I snorted some for the first time. I felt like I had the strength of a thousand men and could sleep with a thousand women and was very focused and ate nothing. I'd spend my time during the week snorting cocaine and drinking just juice, till I was thin as a pencil.

The Tunisians kind of specialized in selling cocaine—the Tunisians and the Moroccans. It was what they did. They came to Italy to deal in it but they never took it. When they saw we were getting wasted, snorting half ourselves and selling the rest, Rashid said, Forget it, work on your own, so we got to know a dealer from Morocco and started getting big amounts of cocaine and hashish from him and selling them off at wholesale prices in Milan and even to Balats 42. We did business with him for around eight months, made lots of money, and took an apartment in a good building in Famagosta and kept the squat just for work. Every night, we'd stay up in the bars and billiard halls till morning. One night, I met my Italian girlfriend. I was playing billiards with el-Zaim and beat him five times. I'd won the game and was sitting there laughing at him. Then I found her looking at me and saying, Why don't you play me instead? I was really happy, put down the chalk that was in my hand, shook hers and said, Saddam the Egyptian! And she said, Toka, which is like "beautiful" in Arabic, and we played. First game she beat me, second game I beat her, third game she beat me, and we sat and had a drink and got to know each other: I'm Egyptian and I work as a plasterer. I'm Italian and I work as a model, and we took each other's phone numbers. The next day, we met at the hall and played and drank and stayed up till morning, and she took me back to the apartment in her Golf. We became friends and she'd come every evening in her car and we'd go and spent the night wherever, and once I invited her over to the apartment. We spent the evening at a disco and went to the apartment and sat and smoked hashish. She asked me, Don't you have any cocaine? Of course I do, and I got her five grams and told her, I'll tell you something new you don't know. I work in drugs. We got high on cocaine and cocaine makes you horny and she was beautiful, like a real honest-to-God model, and it was the summer and we were half naked and I happened to glance at her breasts and felt she'd noticed and I was still trying to hold it together when she said, Would you like to sleep with me?

She was twenty-one and bold and crazy about adventures, and what adventures we had together! Now she's making documentary movies about the drug scene in Italy. Her father had a villa in Sharm el-Sheikh that they rented out for most of the year but she spent every August there. She'd pick up the rent, take a trip to Cairo, do the maintenance, hand it over again to the janitor, and go home. We were together the whole time I was there. She'd leave me when I went into jail and when I came out she'd be the first person to come see me.

One day we'd been drinking at a bar near the Sisyo Centrale and I'd paid and we were leaving. I had one euro left and I put it in the slot-machine and we turned to go. We were at the door when we heard a lot of shouting and balloons going off. It turned out I'd won a hundred euros. I went back to get them, and as I was leaving an Italian guy at a table next to the machine kept waving at me, Play! Play! I put in another euro and won and a third and won till I got up to ten, and then I won a thousand euros and Toka was jumping with joy next to me. I was about to play again when the Italian made a sign with his hand to say, No. I sent him a bottle of wine, and from that day on it was our game, our addiction, and our main craziness.

When a Crown Falls, a Cockerel
Hops on Top of It and Crows

HAJJ MUHAMMAD EL-SEIFAT WAS AN eloquent Bedouin poet and intimate of King Idris el-Senousi, with close ties to the poets and notables of Egypt's Bedouin tribes from one end of the country to the other. When the Leader launched the mighty 1st of September Revolution, he fled to Italy, where he purchased, with the money he'd smuggled out with him, almost half of Italy's Fiat company and led the Libyan opposition to the Leader's coup. He succeeded in destabilizing and threatening the newly born 1st of September Revolution, which was still a bit dumb when it came to governance and administration. In articles in newspapers in the hostile Western media, el-Seifat trained a daily spotlight on the scandals he discovered, not because he was particularly well-informed about the Leader, his revolution, and his family, but because he knew him to be the creature and puppet of the Great Leader, Gamal Abd el-Nasser. And in fact the Leader went on his knees to his mentor and begged him, "Rid us of that man! Let him have whatever he wants, in Libya, or Italy, or even here, in Egypt!" Abd el-Nasser's various secret intelligence services thought the person best suited to negotiate the issue was Bu Bakr el-Basel el-Rumhi, a member of parliament, first because he was a Bedouin and his grandfather had been sheikh of the entire Rimah tribe in Egypt, and second because his other grandfather was Hamad Basha el-Basel, supporter and sturdy bastion of Libya's anti-colonial struggle.

Anyway, el-Basel went to Rome on a mission organized by the Egyptian secret services, met with el-Seifat, and tried convince him to return to Libya and "take whatever he wanted," but el-Seifat had Western protectors and refused, vowing to continue his revolution against the coup d'état to the end. To the Bedouin of the Fayoum he sent, via el-Basel, a *malzuma*—two lines of verse for them to add to, in the traditional Bedouin fashion: the poet writes two lines on some matter that concerns him, such as the loss of a dear friend or beloved, and asks the other poets to add lines. Rumor had it that el-Seifat sent this *malzuma* specifically to a friend of his, the poet of the Rimah tribe in the Fayoum, to ask him whether he thought he should return, and charged el-Basel to deliver it to him with the words "If he indicates that I should return, I will do so." The words of the *malzuma*, however, betray a desire to incite. He urged the Bedouin tribes of Egypt to support the revolution against the young leader, openly urging them to remove him from office. El-Seifat may even have sent it himself, without el-Basel's knowledge. The words are fierce, praising—in the age of the jet plane—bold knights on horseback and muskets:

> *Homeland, to Gaddafi I'll not cede you*
> *Nor to that Upper Egyptian—Never fear, with vengeance I'll feed you!*
> *My vengeance shall come from her east*
> *And all the tribes of Barqa shall ride abreast*
> *Tribes who in neither drinking nor gambling find their ease*
> *Nor ride aught but steeds of perfect form by God—*
> *Steeds that, when the musket shot flies high,*
> *Cast their nails and fight on unshod!*

El-Basel brought the *malzuma* with him to Egypt and handed it over to the secret services. A Bedouin poet from the Fayoum who'd been a friend of el-Seifat's at the height of the Senousi era was summoned and responded with an ode of realism and discouragement, advising him to give up the struggle and go back to Libya to live out his last few days on earth there. The poem tells him that the world has changed and there are no horses or knights or perfect steeds or muskets left, just tanks and jets, and "long-haired kids who strut."

We long for you, Seifat, with honest desire,
Our longing too long unquenched!
Dear friend, precious soulmate,
Come home! Return, like spring, trailing glory from afar
And let us spend a few days more together, mourning the deserted
*   campsites of our past,*
And from what one man has, let all live as one together!
O you who love el-Senousi, O non-pareil,
Surely, rather than stumble, better a man should die?
Where now the muskets?
Where now the men of chivalry and strength
In the days of planes with smoke inside
And armies led by long-haired kids who strut?
It's not the first time that, when a crown falls,
A cockerel hops on top of it and crows.
This is God's way. The universe has always had its rules,
From the days of the Banu Umayya, from the time of King Chosroes.

Loreto

THE MOROCCAN DEALER WOULD HAND over the stuff and settle up with us after we'd taken care of it. Once, he gave us four slabs of hashish worth 500 euros each. We stashed them in the forest close to the Hamlet and they were stolen. Someone saw us bury them and stole them. I owed the Moroccan for eight half-kilos of cocaine so we went to him and told him, The stuff was stolen. Give us something more to work with and wait till we can pay for it. But he refused. He said, Pay what you owe right now. Neither of us would give in but he was an old guy, around forty-five, and I said something and he said something rude back and I hit him, four punches, and he fell down and passed out. El-Zaim told me, Beat it! Now! The district's full of Moroccans and he's the hashish *capo*: he distributes to everyone else. So I left Famagosta altogether and made tracks for Loreto and stayed close to the area with the square where Mussolini was hanged. I put up there with a guy from home called Nemr el-Ghargawi for two days till I found a place with a wrecking contractor and worked with him. I called el-Zaim and he told me he'd made an arrangement with the Moroccan and was getting work from him; there was nothing else the guy could do—he had to give out the goods to get his money back. But el-Zaim hadn't been working for more than two months when one night he was gambling and lost all the money he'd made on the stuff, and the Moroccan came and stabbed him, leaving him with a permanent injury, and the Moroccans gathered and it was like, We're gonna kill you, swear to God! so he ran away and came to me in Loreto. He spent two nights with me, then I took him and put him up in an apartment on the next street over with the bunch from el-Mansoura. He worked with someone as a plasterer and we got out of our old neighborhood completely.

The contractor I was working with was subcontracting from an Italian *capo*, who took a dislike to me the moment he laid eyes on me. He looked me up and down. I looked him up and down. He called me over, very scornfully. I went over, showing my disgust. He said to me, The Arabs are the *terzo mondo*, meaning the backward Third World. I said, Egypt isn't the First World and it isn't the Third World, it's the source of all civilization, and Italy's the *terzo* of Europe. The real clean civilized countries are Germany, Holland, and France. Italy's Euro-trash. He got angry, his face turned red, and he fired me on the spot. I did a few odd plastering jobs with el-Zaim but things were slowing down, there wasn't much work and we'd gotten sick of being laborers anyway, so we fell behind on the rent one month, then two.

The guy who owned the apartment I was living in with el-Zaim didn't throw him out. He thought he'd use him instead to get into the apartment opposite his, which had been empty for a long time so he thought its owners wouldn't be coming back. He let el-Zaim go off to work in the morning, broke into the apartment and changed the lock. When el-Zaim came back he told him he'd bought it and he put el-Zaim in there. Two weeks passed and el-Zaim was going up the stairs one day when he found the police standing there with the real owners and they were throwing his stuff out. He got what was going on immediately. They asked him, Who does this stuff belong to? and he said, I don't know. When the owner of our apartment came, he had a fight with him. If he'd said, Those are my things, he would have gotten at least three years in prison.

There were six of them, not counting the owner, all from el-Mansoura and all working in the same restaurant and each getting two thousand euros a month. They got paid at the end of the month and the same day they'd hand over the whole twelve thousand euros to the owner of the apartment who'd put the money in a locked suitcase under the bed till he could send it to Egypt. They lived off the tips. They worked like hell all through the week and at the weekend each got a girl from the street and they'd have an orgy in the apartment. It was the only good time they had.

They didn't see the street even and drank nothing but water. The apartment owner didn't work. He had two other apartments in addition to that and he lived off them. He used to go to Egypt every three months and turn the goods around, coming and going. He got a girl for himself at the weekend and he took twenty euros for each of the other girls as a hospitality charge—I don't know if he took it from the prostitutes or the tenants. More importantly, he had this regular routine. He'd wake up in the morning at exactly ten, after the others had gone to work, and he'd put on a down-and-dirty Egyptian song and turn up the volume to the max and spend a whole hour in the bathroom. He wouldn't come out even if the whole world was going to pot.

It was this routine he was addicted to that especially tempted el-Zaim. He set off to work with the rest of them in the morning, the way he did every day, and I was waiting for him at the café downstairs. At ten o'clock we went back and he opened the door very carefully and we went in and found the owner exactly as usual, with a song by Hasan el-Asmar on at top volume while he made a racket in the bathroom. El-Zaim pulled the suitcase out from under the bed and we went off to the squat in Porta Genova, where I'd got nabbed, and into the forest and opened it. In it we found twelve thousand euros in all their glory, plus six Egyptian passports with their Italian papers and the apartment owner's checkbook.

We made a bonfire of the passports and the papers in the forest and took the money and the checkbook and went back to my apartment. At the end of the day, el-Zaim rejoined them at the apartment, covered with cement dust, looking like he was coming back from work as normal.

We blew the money in two months—drugs, gambling, and bars till morning. There was a thousand euros left, so we spoke to Rashid in Famagosta and he came and took them and gave us two *qirsh*es of hashish and we sat and sold them in the garden at Loreto for two days. Then we found ourselves surrounded by a gang of Albanians with jackknives—Wassup? Not much. They said it was their territory and nobody could come near it. Fine, buddy, let us work with you! We can't trust you and you have to get out of here, that's it. The Albanians are very dangerous. They're Italy's real Mafia. They'll kill you for fun.

So, there was nothing to do but leave the whole territory to them.

Blessed by a Miracle

HAMDAN IS CONSIDERED TO HAVE been blessed, though the miracle was really his overly trusting, or perhaps overly bathed, mother's and only his by inheritance. Hamdan was the nephew of Wahba, the Nubian, our neighbor back home. He left in the seventies and, given that he'd always been bright and energetic and had been raised among us and knew the Bedouin dialect as well as the Bedouin themselves, he presented himself as a Rumhi from the Fayoum and obtained a Saad-Shin card after his first interview in the Benghazi office. He sent home a recorder and a tape in which he prattled away in the dialect like any Bedouin sheikh, letting everyone know he was fine and working in contracting.

A few months later, though, war broke out. The Egyptian army swept through Libya up to the borders with Tunisia and all news of Hamdan was lost. Aunt Aziza went crazy and cried herself blind, so she went to the sheikh and the headman and even the officer at the police station time and again but received no news of the boy to give her hope. In the end, she decided to "open a book" for him (our village was famous for "opening books," with always at least three people there at any one time who could open you one) and Aunt Aziza did the ceremony with the most skillful of them, Uncle Bekheit, to whom she took something Hamdan had worn (an undershirt, I think, or an old pair of drawers) and asked him to cast a spell that would bring him back. Sheikh Bekheit made his conjurations over the rag and burned his incense, but instead of presenting her with a spell, he gave her a set of instructions: she was to bathe before dawn, go up onto the roof of her house naked, and call, or better still scream at the top of her voice, "Hamdaaan!" three times, and Hamdan would hear her wherever he was and come back, God willing.

Uncle Wahba said his wife had gone crazy. He said it to himself and he said it to her: the boy had driven her nuts. "You'll make a public scandal of us! What are people going to say when they see you stark naked and screaming away like that in the middle of the night?"

But Aziza was desperate with longing. "My heart breaks for my son, but my son's heart breaks not for me!" she cried, and one night she gave her husband the slip, bathed late at night, and climbed up, stark naked, before the dawn prayer had been called, onto the roof, where she put her hands behind her ears, like a muezzin, and sang out, at the top of her voice, "Hamdan! Hamdaaan!"

No one knows whether it was coincidence or whether he really heard her out there in the deserts of Libya but two days later he was back. Hamdan came back and he came back in better shape than he'd left. The whole town watched him riding in the white Peugeot station wagon, its roof crowned with bags. And, given that he'd returned without facing any difficulties at the height of the armed clash between the Egyptian and Libyan leaders, it seems he thought he could return any time, so after two months he went back to Libya. But that time he didn't return. Aziza cried herself blind and her voice shattered the quiet of our village nights time and again, but Hamdan never came back.

Thanks to his Saad-Shin card, he found work with a company drilling for gas in the deserts around Sirte. When the Libyan secret intelligence services officer came to the company and took the names and addresses of every Saad-Shin it employed, he got scared they were going to conscript him into the army, so he ran away from Sirte entirely, to the homeland of the Saad-Shin in Sabha.

The Station

WE TOOK THE TRAIN TO Porta Romana and went to a bunch of Fayoum Bedouin guys from home who were staying on Cors el-Lodi at the old train station, which has large grounds—fifteen or twenty hectares—in the middle of the forest. It's been abandoned for years, only one train goes through it, and it has large outbuildings next to the tracks on both sides where people from all over the world live—Africans, Moroccans, Tunisians, Albanians, Romanians, Egyptians. Each group had cleared the garbage and crap from a building, mopped it out well, put beds and mattresses on the floors, and set themselves up there.

Our relations were living in one of the buildings and would spend the night lying in wait in the forest for the drug dealers. Everyone working in drugs in Milan stashed their stuff there, and my relations would stay up late lying on their bellies waiting for someone to come along and stash stuff. As soon as he'd done it and taken off, they'd rush out and dig around till they found it. Often, they'd come across a couple of stashes in one night but sometimes a week or even a whole month would go by without them finding even one. A batch of cocaine, a package of hashish, or some stolen goods—that was the sort of stuff they did. Breakfast, lunch, and dinner were at the church and, of course, they slept at the old station for free. The moment they saw me, they shook in their shoes. They knew me from home and knew what I'd gotten up to here too. They made us welcome, yes, but their embarrassment and unhappiness were obvious. We stayed for two days. Then on the third, on my way into the station, I noticed a building made of corrugated iron. It was inside the station, sure, but you had to walk all the way to the end to get to it. It was tiled and had a door but was stacked with wine bottles. I got el-Zaim and we cleaned it out, straightened it up well, got our belongings and settled down inside. At night we'd light it with a candle and during the day it was God's own daylight.

We kept looking for work but there wasn't any, not even in hashish. I was known and my smell was everywhere in Italy. I'd run from the stink in Egypt and, lo and behold, the stink was waiting for me wherever I went. But that was OK with me. I like staying up all night and drinking and gambling and life, and I'd only come to Italy so I could do that without troubles, and here I was, living my life, praise God! You could say to anyone, Muhyi Bu Musa, and he'd say, God protect us! You could say, Azam Abdallah Sfeit, and he'd jump. You could say, El-Baffo Saddam the Egyptian and he'd say, You want to put me in jail or what?

One of my older cousins had close friends who were big *capo*s in Milan. One of them was like the Emperor of Scaffolding for the whole city: all the scaffolding you saw on the buildings throughout Milan belonged to him. Another was the biggest contractor doing house and apartment building façades in the whole of Milan. Both were from near us in Tatoun hamlet, which had a whole nation resident in Milan—there were whole neighborhoods called Tatoun. I went to them on a Monday and they all welcomed me well and stuck their hands into their pockets and pulled out a thousand euros and, like, Take these till you find work, but when I kept it up and began phoning people ten times a day, Hajj Muhammad, the scaffolding guy, answered me with a few words that were clear and to the point: What are you trying to do, son? Put us to work for you? Your own uncle told us you were trouble. Our work's out there on the street for anyone to steal and we aren't prepared to throw away another three or four million just to make you happy.

So there was no way out except drugs. (That was then, of course. Today, we don't even have drugs.) We did well and became the lords of all Famagosta. Toka and I made it a rule only to spend the night in the bars where the stars of society went and we played at the same table as Berlusconi, the prime minister.

Back then, though, we were hungry, and I mean really, really hungry. I thought eating at the church was disgusting. Not the food itself, but the crowding and the lines and the women. The women there were my countrywomen, Egyptians—you could tell them from their headscarves—and when I saw them I wanted to sink into the ground. They weren't just the poor and the washed-up like me. There were guys who earned five thousand euros a month and made their wives—or whose wives made themselves—get three meals a day from the church, and force their way in and get squashed and rubbed up against by all the men, the Albanians, the Romanians, and, of course, the Egyptians, till they got their food.

We spent some time robbing supermarkets. You go into a big supermarket. You find what you want—food and drink, the finest kinds of alcohol—shove it under your jacket and leave. I used to wear a jacket that looked like it was made for stealing. Of course there are cameras but the mineral-water corner didn't have any. You tore off the label on whatever it was and bought yourself something or other for camouflage. I got caught lots of times. They'd take whatever it was and tell you to get out of there. Once I was hungry and went into a supermarket where I'd been caught before and took a grilled chicken and a bottle of wine and sat down and ate in the middle of the store. Security came and very politely took me, with my bottle of wine and my chicken, to eat in a side room.

Easier and safer than supermarkets was stealing bicycles. A large new pair of cutters and, *scrunch!*, the bike's yours. You could sell a bike just by standing around in the Porta Genova market. Plus some mugging: mugging the drunks coming out of the bars at the end of the night, especially black Americans who drank with us, because they'd be so drunk and out of it as we shook them down. One would stagger out of a bar, you'd hug him, hold him tight with your arms, and shake him down while he laughed. Some, though, would balk and go crazy and run, yelling insults at "the Moroccans"—Thieving Moroccans! Thieving Moroccans! The Moroccans were like the American blacks. They'd drink till they were legless. But the Moroccans were hard as nails, and stubborn, and they'd fight to the death for a five-piaster coin. El-Zaim, "Tweezers" the Tunisian, and I would walk around at dawn, from three to five. The Tunisian was called Tweezers because he was a pickpocket. He could steal the mascara off your eyelids. By that time of night, people have gotten totally drunk and are on their way home. We'd see one come swaying along and we'd grab him. Obviously, there wouldn't be any resistance. I'd grab one by the back of his neck and say, Keep your trap shut and hand over everything you've got! He'd hand it all over as meek as a mouse. Once el-Zaim and I mugged a guy and took 42,000 euros off him. We spent them in a week on gambling.

We did a bit too in Biyassa Trenta—Garden No. 30—in Famagosta, right next to the station. It's Milan's gay garden. A guy will come in his luxury car and find a gallery of young Arabs—Moroccans, Tunisians, Egyptians—all ready and waiting. He agrees on a price with one of them and they do it wherever. Poor gays didn't go to Biyassa Trenta—it'd be death and destruction: they'd get their pockets emptied and be beaten up.

I was taken there by Toba, a kid of my age from Ebshaway. He was the boyfriend of Umm Toba, who was a Romanian woman who thought of him as her son. He slept with her, obviously, but it was understood that he was her son, so we used to address her as Umm Toba. I saw Lame Fathi there in the garden, working, I mean like really working—his pants down and sticking his thing out and showing it off all round the garden.

Fathi had had polio. When he walked, he supported his weight by holding on to his knee with his hand, but he was as strong as an ox. I found the whole thing disgusting. Plus it wasn't worth it—a hundred euros and not a cent more.

When we were living at the station, before we moved to the villa, I came in one day and found Toba with his girlfriend, a beautiful Italian girl from Sicily aged around thirty-five. It was the first time I'd seen her and I thought she was one of those girls who do it for money. I asked him, Business?

He said, If you can get her to.

I told him, Fine, leave us alone for a bit, so he left. I sat down with her. A chat plus a laugh plus a cigarette and we were done.

Benghazi

LIBYA WAS OPEN. THE LEADER himself had driven the bulldozer and demolished the gateway at the border post with Egypt, and the young men who were my neighbors and from my clan were leaving on an almost daily basis. I, though, went to el-Minya, so that I could leave from there. I don't know why I expected it would be better to go with guys from el-Minya as far as getting work and making money in Libya were concerned (or perhaps, to be honest, I knew that the Fayoum people were the laziest anywhere). I took a per-person Toyota minibus with Naji, my colleague from school and the army. It left from el-Edwa, in the district of Maghagha, and went north till it got to El Alamein, then west to Salloum. When it got to Libya, I started to feel afraid.

A barren desert. What kind of work was I supposed to find here? It really was a sandbox, as Mussolini had said. This must be the region where Umar el-Mukhtar had set his terrible trap for the Italian army.

We got to Benghazi at the end of the night and it was totally empty. Wide, shiny-clean streets bathed in street lighting, the only thing to be seen our eyes peering out of the Toyota. Suddenly, a police siren sounded and we heard a voice shout, "You, boy! Hold it right there, dumbass!" and a police van swerved out in front of us. A high-end vehicle, latest model, gleaming and lighting up the whole place, and with an amazing aerial, very long and waving about in a lordly fashion as though threatening everyone. A black officer, about fifty years old, got out along with two policemen no less black and tall. He wrenched open the door of the minibus, looked at us in great disgust, and said, "Piss pants!" I think he almost spat, or maybe did spit, in our faces. He poked a few of us with a prod he was holding and said, "You think anything goes here, like in Egypt? You're going straight to the interrogation room." Then he looked at the driver with a disgusted expression and said, "Follow me, piss pants!"

We followed along behind him, he entered a police station, and they took the driver, who came back about two hours later so badly beaten he was coughing up blood. It turned out we'd crashed a red light and it was all just an eloquent Libyan lesson for the nonchalant Egyptian driver. Naturally, given the driver's condition and our having been cooped up so long in the minibus, we stayed that night in Benghazi, in the open, in a desert area in the middle of the city. We woke to a light rain and set off south for Zliten.

We reached Zliten after about three hours and were met by my colleague's relatives and acquaintances, most of whom worked on farms or as shepherds in the mountains. What jobs there were were to be found at the hireling market. You went there and then it was up to God. I discovered that we were already standing in the market when a pickup stopped and was stormed by an army of laborers, including two of the people who'd been talking to us. I made up my mind to go on to Sabha. Here it was total crap and, what with my family and my clan, I'd been through enough crap already. So I set off for Sabha.

The Battle with the Tunisians

THE TUNISIANS WERE FIVE WILD kids who lorded it over the people living in the station. One day el-Zaim got into a fight with them. He threatened them and they threatened him, on the railroad tracks. His three cousins came so we pulled out our cudgels and climbed up onto the track. Then, suddenly, the Tunisians gave a yell and rushed us, so el-Zaim and his relations fled faster than you can say "jackknife" and left me all alone surrounded by five gleaming machetes, and one of these swung back, shone in the air, and slammed down onto me, right above my eye. I only came round in the hospital. The Tunisians thought I was dead and they gathered up their stuff from the station and vanished, and I went back and became the *capo* of the station. After our battle with the Tunisians, I became known at the station as el-Baffo, meaning "the bald guy with the mustache," and I made one hell of a *baffo*: I shaved off my hair with a razor, grew my mustache, wore an Inter Milan T-shirt, and called myself el-Baffo Saddam. El-Baffo Saddam the Egyptian, who scared even the police.

(The Phantom Raider's official name is Ihab and he's known as Muhyi, and throughout his career he's taken many other titles and names. At this period it seems he got fed up with being so well known, or at his failure to hide his glaring failure, so he decided to play the fool, shaved his head, grew a mustache like the handlebar of a Nasr bicycle, and took to wearing an Inter Milan T-shirt. Even the Italian police officers used to call him el-Baffo.)

I began doing business with Balats 42, which supplied drugs to the whole of Italy, and there was nothing the police could do about it. It was close to us in Porta Romana—an old, five-sided, apartment building, with a fifty-meter façade, two sides of around twenty-five meters this way and twenty-five meters that, then another twenty-five, then the door, then another twenty-five. It was built exactly like a hospital—three wings, each three stories tall and divided into apartments, each apartment consisting of one room and a bathroom. Everyone who lived there was Egyptian, and when I'd been working at Famagosta with the Moroccan, I'd been distributing to all the guys who worked there, so the moment they saw me in the entrance they gathered round and it was all hugs, and Muhammad Elyan, the sheikh of the Bedouins who worked there, took me to his apartment on the third floor. I spent the night at his place and the next day he gave me a hundred grams of heroin and I went back to the squat and began working.

The Leader Gets Fed Up

As I've said earlier, Nobel Prize-winning novelist Llosa wrote his famous novel *The Feast of the Goat* about a Latin American dictator, but all the fantasies and the insanities of that mad dictator were nothing compared to the real-life doings of the Leader and his career, which would have been more appropriate to a prophet, or at least someone somehow or other "blessed."

He saw himself as a prophet and generally addressed the Prophet of God as an equal, or associate. He also had opinions and interpretations of scripture that were enough to make the fundamentalists call him an infidel. These included viewing the Prophet's migration to Medina, which Muslims consider a cause for celebration and a patent victory, as simply a defeat and an ignominious flight, which it is shameful to take as the starting point of the Islamic era; we ought, rather, to begin with the conquest of Mecca. And he came up, all on his own, with an extraordinary calendar in which he named the months after the sea, sun, water, and Hannibal, which was also what he called his son, the Hannibal who's now on the run in some country or other.

Many Libyans believed that the Leader had indeed been granted semi-divine powers. As a boy studying in second-year middle school, he agreed with his classmates that they would bring about the 1st of September Revolution and overthrow the Senousi king, this being the lesson he'd learned from Egypt and its Nasserist revolution and Boss-Commander-Leader. And that is exactly what happened. The Leader entered Sabha middle school, along with his classmates. From there they went to military high school, from there to military college, and from there to direct rule over Libya, for forty-two years, during which he tried out all the bizarre ideas of his "international theory," as preserved, like scripture, in *The Green Book*. "I don't rule Libya. Libya is ruled by the Popular Committees": thus sayeth the Leader, expounding from *The Green Book*. "The age of governments is over, and power is in the hands of the people." According to this Third International Theory, the Great State of the Masses is ruled by the masses; before the Leader, there were two international theories of governance—the socialist and the capitalist—and both failed and continued to fail throughout the decades, until the long-awaited Third International Theory appeared, ushering in "the age of the masses."

Unfortunately, though, his theory foundered, in turn, on the rock of the indifference of the Great Libyan People, who ended up killing him. He—or the theory— told them, "Weapons belong in the hands of the people," which was an idea truly worthy of a prophet and does indeed offer a solution to our plight, I swear, an end to the era of rapacious armies and the emergence of an age of the just masses. This was what led the Leader to invent the name "the Great Socialist People's Libyan Arab State of the Masses" for his country. But when it came to applying the idea, and once the Libyan families had received the boxes of arms and ammunition that had belonged to the Libyan army, civil war broke out, the weapons were stacked in reception rooms and every little quarrel between neighbors turned into a deadly battle waged with automatics to which any member of the warring parties might fall victim.

The Green Book said, "The house belongs to the one who lives in it!" which is indeed what everyone dreams of: suddenly one morning, you find yourself owner of the house you've been renting, or of the apartment you've been living in, and the age of landlord and renter is over. Likewise, "No hirelings or hired hands!" But when the dream was implemented in real life, it turned into tragedy, with bloody stories of families who returned to their houses and apartments only to find others—occupiers, in fact—holding up to them the slogan of *The Green Book*, in green letters: "The house belongs to him who lives in it!"

Despite which he hung on, adopting whatever form he had to, the last being that of the Thinker: "I am neither commander nor president. I do not rule Libya. Libya is ruled by the Committees. I am naught but a man who calls for revolution!" However, the revolution for which he called throughout his life never materialized, though that is another story.

At the end of his days, the Leader grew fed up with his recalcitrant people. He began to feel that they were too few for him, or hadn't lived up to his expectations. He upbraided them on the radio and the television, upfront and to their faces: "I swear I don't know what to do with you! You don't deserve our national systems!" To be honest, he was right about some things, which is sad, of course. But that's how I see it myself, and now he's dead, so one can talk openly. Colonel el-Gaddafi, never mind the outcomes or the stupidity or the fundamental tyranny, was sincere about his socialist revolution and about placing the people's resources in their own hands, but all his ideas for giving them power over their own wealth and weapons foundered on the rock of their stubborn Bedouin indifference.

Needless to say, the Leader himself was a living embodiment of the revolutionary Arab Nationalist liberation regimes that expelled colonialism and imposed on the Arab peoples something more injurious and severe than any colonialism. Before him, Libya wasn't a country: it was three administrative areas or regions that the United Nations united under the crown of el-Senousi, who formerly had reigned over Barqa only. Not to mention that his long-awaited revolutionary regime of the Age of the Masses provided everything, from A to Z, to those masses, from home to summer holiday home, at the state's expense.

The House of Abundance

WHEN I WAS SITTING IN the room we'd cleaned out at the old Cors el-Lodi station, I saw eight Romanians, four women and four men, who used to go around selling smuggled Romanian cigarettes and stealing at the Sisyo Centrale, Milan's main station. At the end of the day, they'd return, go down the side of the old station, and jump over the wall of the house at the end. Next morning, they'd come out again. I found it difficult to sleep at the station, so I lit a joint and thought, These people go out in the morning and come back at the end of the day to sleep, so what's in there? And I jumped over the wall and found a villa, I mean like a real villa—furniture, water, light, and people living there normally—but they'd locked the door to the outside. Not the door in the wall, but the villa's front door, which they never opened. Instead, they'd go out by the back door, jump over the wall, enter the old station, walk to its main gate, go through it to the outside, and continue to the Sisyo Centrale. That way, no one knew they were living there.

The moment I saw it, I said, That's mine. I'm taking that villa and that's all there is to it, and I went back and got Toba and three of our relatives and we picked up the Romanians' clothes and stuff and moved it outside the wall, inside the old station. When they came at the end of the day, they found us sitting there stark naked, each of us with a blade as long as he was tall in his hand. Okay! Okay! they told us. We don't want trouble, and they took their stuff and left.

We stayed one month, then another, in the villa but never opened the front door. When we finally did, we found a garden that was all grass, its edges lined with ficus trees, which formed a kind of wall, five meters high. It was big enough to park around five cars belonging to the company next door to the villa. Behind the villa was another garden, with grapes, plums, apples, roses, and jujubes. One day, as I was sitting at sunset in front of the door to the villa, on the grass, and lighting up a joint, I suddenly saw someone come in, open the door to a Cherokee jeep that was parked there, and climb in. When he saw me, he got out again, came over, and asked, *Buono? Questo è buono?* meaning, Is that good hashish? So I said, *Troppo buono*—Too good! He said, *Posso provare?*—May I try? I told him, Go ahead. He took it, smoked about half the joint, got stoned, and asked me, Do you have any more and I said, *Sì*. He asked me, *Quantita?*—How much have you got? I said, *Ma chi sei?*—Who are you to ask? so he laughed and said, Don't worry about me. I'm not the police, I own this place. Before you, there were Romanians staying here. They were afraid to open the door but you Arabs are tough, you opened the door and came out into the garden. Then he told me, I want a quarter slab. I thought I'd try him out so I said, Five hundred euro, but he laughed and said, No way! A whole slab's five hundred euro. Are you trying to cheat me? Don't think you can get *furbo* with me! So I went inside, got him the quarter, and said, Here! He was getting his money out but I told him, No, it's a present from me to you. We're living in your house after all, my friend. He said, No, it's not my house, it's yours. Then he took the quarter and left.

And we set to work. We'd bring the hashish from the forest, from the Moroccan in Famagosta: you'd go into the forest and find two Moroccans stopping you going any further. Who do you want? I'd tell them, I want Rashid the Moroccan. They'd go and speak to Rashid and tell him, It's Saddam the Egyptian. He'd tell them, Let him pass, and you'd go and pay and get your share and go back and cut it up into *qirsh*s, or fingers, and sell. We kept this up for a while.

One of my customers was a Brazilian thief called Andrea. We got to know one another and became friends. He began bringing the best of what he'd stolen and I'd take what I wanted—phones, watches, gold chains, stuff like that. I'd invite him and his girlfriend out and they'd invite me to their house, and we'd go to the disco. Once I was at their place and I got a hard-on for his girlfriend. She was white and tall and had green eyes and an incredible body. We'd just blown cocaine, so I said, Andrea, I'm sorry but I want to sleep with your girlfriend. He laughed and said, Tell her! So I said the same to her and she said, Me too. I've wanted to sleep with you for ages. So I took her by the hand while Andrea laughed and we went into the bedroom. We began to kiss and undress each other and I went down on my knees and pulled down her panties and something jerked out— *trakk!*—in my face. It turned out he was a man, with a schlong yea big!

In the end, Rashid got arrested. They mounted a raid against him in the forest and he was shot in the leg and caught. With him they seized thirty-two cartons of hashish, half a kilo of cocaine, and half a kilo of heroin. You know how long he got for that? Just five years! That's because they really value freedom there, and if you go to prison they give you an allowance of five euros a day and the prison itself is like a hotel compared to the ones in Egypt. The cells are for six persons and have six beds and there's a TV with 1600 channels. You can watch Indian, Arabic, rude stuff, anything you want. Every week you get a DVD you can keep overnight so you can see videos of your family, your loved ones, whatever you like. In the end it was still a prison, though, even if there were lots of Egyptians who'd do anything to get inside one when they were down on their luck.

Anyway, the main thing is Rashid was caught and we began looking for another dealer. I came across a guy in a bashed-up old moving van that was parked in the street. I was walking past when I smelled hashish. Right away I banged on the window and a guy opened it. I said, Hi! Egyptian? He said, Egyptian. I asked him, Where from? He said, The Fayoum. I said, Where exactly? He said, Tatoun. I told him, I'm from el-Gharg. Why are you sleeping rough? He said, I just got out of jail and haven't found anywhere to sleep yet. I told him, OK. Pick up your stuff and come with me.

I took him with me to the villa and put him up there with me, Hazem, and Toba. At that point, I was still jumping over the wall. Then me and the owner of the house became friends and, hey presto, he gave me the key for the small door, the door to the big garage where the cars were. This small door, which we got the key for, was the one we took to using.

Another time I got to know another guy. His name was Ashraf Bu Naasa, from Tatoun too. He was a cocaine addict and snorted it a lot. Even though it was me who'd brought the bunch to the house, I was scared of them. I'd get up early—it didn't matter how late I'd stayed up, I'd get up early because I had just one wish during my life there, what with the squats, the fear, and the drugs: I hoped and I prayed and I begged the Lord, Before I die, please let me sleep one night without fear! I'd get high on a couple of joints and I'd sit on my own and cry over how my life was: It has to be this way, it's no use trying to live any other way, this is the only way I know how to live. I'd have died if I'd come into the country to be a respectable type and lived off the churches and hadn't done anything wrong—I'd have died! I know lots of Egyptians who haven't done a thing wrong from the moment they arrived. The moment they wake in the morning they have breakfast at the church, they have lunch at the church, they get their clothes from the church—a life not fit for a dog. I can't live like that. Muhyi Bu Musa, who was a daredevil in Egypt and managed to get by even if he had to steal, wasn't the type to live that life. So I got into drugs and went for it.

I'd sit on my own and smoke a couple of joints and look at the sky and cry. I cried because I was scared my goods would get stolen. I was scared the police would pop up out of nowhere and find goods on me and I'd go to prison. I was scared some Moroccans or Tunisians would attack me with cleavers and knives and take everything I had—twenty or thirty at a go, what are you going to do against them? Right behind where you're staying there's a waste ground where there's everybody—Moroccans, Africans, Albanians, Romanians, and God knows who else. And from the day we threw the Romanians out of the place we're living in, other people had had their eye on it—a whole villa, and great-looking? We were so scared we didn't go in by the station door. Instead we'd opened the outside door, the one that gave straight onto the street.

I'd smoke a couple of joints and sit alone and feel like, I don't know—like you want to go home but you can't: you haven't made any money. Everything you get is spent on drugs and you haven't sent anything back to your family so you can go back there. Go back to what? And, anyway, time's up, you're older now. What are you going do there? So you go on living in this wasteland, always on-edge, on-edge about every-thing. A strange land, and no one to get your back.

Hashish over there makes you think stuff you can't imag-ine, like, OK, if I get killed here, how will my family take revenge? And who from, and who'd know anyway? I wouldn't amount to a hill of beans: I'd be just a dog that had slunk off somewhere.

Eweidat and His Feuds

FINALLY I REMEMBER HIS NAME! Eweidat el-Hasnawi was the owner of the workshop. He was really kind and really cantankerous. Tall, thin, brown, and a little stooped. A retired headmaster. He was the kind of Libyan who considered the Leader and the revolutionary leadership a bunch of thieves but he kept it under his hat and never breathed a word, not even to a Saad-Shin. He thought of himself and his tribe, the Hasnawiya, as the lords of Sabha and resented the savages who'd taken it over. Most of all, he resented the Gaddafi tribe, and most of all among those the Leader, but in a silence that sometimes gave rise to unjustified irascibility, aggression, and suspicion. He hated "the fake-Libyan Saad-Shins who roam the town pretending to be Libyans but who're just scum in Egypt. If they weren't scum, they'd never have left Egypt and come here." His hatred for them usually gave further rise to slanders against Egypt itself, and the moment he learned that Egypt, the country, isn't mentioned in the Qur'an, he was like, "The *misr* mentioned in the verse that says, 'Get you down to "a" *misr*!' is another *misr*. It doesn't mean the *misr* that is Egypt, it means any old *misr*! Plus Egypt isn't 'the Mother of the World'! Who says it's the Mother of the World?" along with sarcastic comments such as "If Egypt's the mother of the world, who's its father?" and, of course, all the stuff about the peace treaty with Israel and the Great Betrayal. Abd el-Aziz and Abd el-Slam would always take his side and go like, "How did those people get to be raised that way?" plus a sometimes near-kamikaze enthusiasm for the Palestinian cause and a near-complicit silence over the miserable state of our personal causes—freedom, security, and personal independence. The entire Arab people has gone half a century fighting for the Palestinian cause while being governed, as though it didn't matter, by the stupidest and least successful despots witnessed by humanity in the modern age.

Abd el-Aziz and Abd el-Slam always took Eweidat's side, with Egypt on trial in the restaurant, but I'd silence their arguments, falling on them with the utmost vehemence, stupidity, and desire to lord it over them and be offensive: "Hatred of Egypt is the natural response of the primitive to civilization and the city, of the backward to the evolved, of the poorest children on the street to its only wealthy offspring," and I'd go to great lengths to shove in their faces the dictatorship, the repression, the interrogation rooms, and the king before whom they prostrate themselves to this day.

Anyway, one day Eweidat woke up and the workshop was nowhere to be found. "I took my eye off the workshop and the restaurant and that bastard sold them and made a run for Tunisia." His partner, Hadi the Tunisian, had sold the equipment and the clients' cars. This was something totally normal in Libya—not the theft and the way it was done (which was totally Tunisian) but the ease with which such stolen property could be sold. It was perfectly normal to find someone who'd buy off you an armed vehicle belonging to the armed forces. Two of my Saad-Shin friends sold the trucks they drove while they were in the army, went to Egypt, and then came back as though it was the most natural thing in the world. They came back to Libya and even went back into the army, after an officer from Gaddafi's tribe interceded for them.

So Eweidat came on his weekly visit to the workshop and couldn't find it. He went crazy. It was to be expected that he'd go a little crazy and rave and ask God to do something about it, but Eweidat the Stubborn hung in there and focused and followed Hadi to Tunis, where he asked around till they brought Hadi to him from his family's house, and he got back everything that had been stolen, through his tribal ties and without the help of the relevant authorities or even informing them.

Biyassa Trenta

ANYWAY, HAZEM, KARIM, TOBA, AND Ashraf Bu Naasa were left with me at the villa, and after Rashid got caught we almost starved to death. One day I met one of the Tunisians living next to us in the station and he told me about a factory nearby in the forest that they stole copper from and sold for twenty euros a kilo to a rag-and-bone man who gave you cash.

That night, I got the guys together, handed everyone a box-cutter, a saw, and a travel bag, and we went and jumped over the wall and found an abandoned car factory with large copper cables in it. We worked away at them all night long with the saws and cutters, and by the morning each of us had filled his bag with wire. We dragged the bags away and handed them to one another over the wall, and we got on the bus and went to the rag-and-bone man just as he was opening for the day, and he weighed the stuff and paid us.

We lived like that for about a month, each making five or six hundred euro a night, which he'd go and spend on slot machines and cocaine. Then one day Hatem Bu el-Mazzaz came and told me he'd seen Ali Balaha, who supplied Balats 42 with drugs, stashing something away in the irrigation ditch. Behind the station there's a road and on the other side of the road there are buildings and people living, in a very quiet neighborhood, and in the middle of the buildings there's an irrigation ditch with thick esparto grass and trees growing out of it. I went with him and he searched around under a tree and found a package. We grabbed it, took a roundabout route back through the forest, and returned to the squat. We reckoned it would be cocaine but it turned out to be a half of heroin, which we didn't know how to sell and didn't do ourselves, so we took it and stashed it in the forest and forgot about it.

Later, I got to know a Moroccan on Carlo Farini. We were talking about goods and stuff and how I didn't have any money, and he said, Come with me and I'll give you something and you can pay me back when you've unloaded it. So the first time I took half a slab from him and I paid him back, and the second I took a whole slab but I spent the money on the slot machines and he wouldn't give me any more, and the only thing left was Biyassa Trenta.

Biyassa Trenta is opposite the House of Abundance on the other side of the station wall. It's known as the main pickup place for gays in Milan. All day long, Moroccans, Tunisians, and Egyptians show themselves off to them and one of them comes and makes a circuit in his car and when he finds someone he likes he calls to him and tells him to get in next to him and they agree on the money and go and do it wherever. Once, when I was coming back from the bar, I saw Fathi Laaraj resting on his crutch with his thing out, rubbing it stiff and waving it about in front of everybody, so I went up to him and pretended to be a fellow Moroccan and said, What do you think you're doing? He got scared and told me, I'm sorry, buddy, it's just work. I told him, Fuck that. Don't do it again, OK? He said, OK, and that night I found that Toba had brought him to me at the squat.

Once I saw a man and woman there making the circuit in their car. I was just thinking, What brings them here? when they waved to me and I got in with them. The man turned to me and asked me, Is your thing big? I said, What's it to do with you? He said, This woman's my wife and she wants to get fucked, so how about you fuck her? But I like to watch her getting fucked. So we agreed on the money and they took me with them. They took me to a luxury flat next to the Domo church and she dragged me quickly and urgently into the bedroom and we did it while he watched us through the keyhole. When I came out I found him covered with sweat, and instead of the hundred we'd agreed he gave me two hundred.

Anyway, the main thing is, I worked it out with the gang, stuck out my chest, and walked around Biyassa Trenta. A guy stopped in a brand-new Golf—how much? so much—and we agreed on a hundred euro and I got in with him. He asked me, Do you know a place? so I told him the place we'd fixed on, behind the buildings on a bit of bare land in the fields next to a shack. As soon as he turned on the light inside the car and began feeling me up, the gang attacked and it was like, Freeze! Freeze! and Hand over everything you've got! while he sat there terrified. I pretended to put up a fight but he told me, Give it to them! Give it to them! And they took two thousand euro off him, plus a watch, a chain, and a cell phone. I told him they'd taken five hundred euro of mine and a watch and a cell phone, so he went to an ATM and took out two thousand euro and gave them to me. Then we agreed we'd meet at his apartment and took each other's numbers. But, screw it, I didn't see him again. I went back to the gang and we divided up the money.

I took the cell phone and went to see the Moroccan on Carlo Farini. I told him to deduct the slab of hashish I owed him and give me another. He pulled open the drawer of a bedside table where there were at least thirty slabs of hashish neatly arranged, crammed the phone into it, and gave me a slab. As I was about to leave, he said, Wait, I'll go down with you, I have something to do in Loreto. We left the building and he got into a taxi, and I went back to Mahmoud el-Saidi, who was waiting for me in the garden. We talked about it, then went back to the Moroccan's building and waited in front till one of the residents left. I pretended to be talking on my phone and said, Forget it, forget it, don't open, there's someone coming out, and we went in. The building had three apartments per story and the Moroccan was living on the first. I stepped back and it took only one kick right on the lock for the door to fall out of its frame. We ran to the drawer of the bedside table and loaded up the hashish, the cell phone, a hundred and fifty euro, and a big ball of something I didn't recognize, and snuck out.

Mahmoud was short and kind of agile and he was wearing a sweat suit and looked like a child so I made him walk in front of me with the bag till we got to the subway station. I was still buying the tickets to Cors el-Lodi when I saw him jump over the ticket machines and get on the train that was leaving. I couldn't catch up with him so I got on the next and got out at Cors el-Lodi. There were lots of police so I took a short cut to the House of Abundance and got there before him. When he got there he called out to the guys inside. I ran over to him and put my hand over his mouth and took him to the garden, where we took out one slab and buried the bag with the rest of the stuff. We split the slab among the gang. The ball I hadn't recognized turned out to be a half-kilo of cocaine.

Once I went out on my own. Someone picked me up, we agreed on the money, and I told him to call me after I finished work. I went and got a cleaver and stuck it down the back of my shirt. He called me and took me to a car dealership in Loreto so we could do it and he could give me a hundred euro, and the moment he came close to me, I whipped my hand over my shoulder, pulled out the cleaver, and stuck him up, like, Open the safe, and he opened it and took out forty thousand euro, which I snatched from him. I told him, Not a move! and escaped into the street, changed the SIM card, and never saw him again.

San Fakturya

WE GOT TO KNOW ALI Balaha, an Egyptian who dealt in cocaine and heroin, and began taking a kilo or two at a time from him on consignment and selling it in the building and the gardens. The money rolled in and we began dressing well and eating well. Every day we were in the bars and at the slot machines, and each week the owner of the house would come by and take a quarter slab of hashish and go. Once the police raided us as he was leaving and we had the stuff with us. They'd just stopped us and begun searching the house when he came running back, shouting, Hey! Hey! Hey! What do you think you're doing? That's my house. What's your business here? The head guy said, These guys are dealing drugs. The owner said, You have no right to enter the house without my knowledge and without going through me. Please be so good as to leave. And off they went, leaving us with the kilo of cocaine that had been right under their noses.

All of us began snorting cocaine. We'd move half and snort the other half in the lab. Beneath the villa there was a basement with broken steps. When you looked down into it you saw garbage. There was a terrible smell but there were rooms there and we'd go down by rope and use it to cut cocaine. Once while we were cutting it, me, Ashraf Bu Naasa, and Toba, a customer phoned Bu Naasa. He'd just bought two grams of cocaine from him and wanted two more. Ashraf told Toba, Go up and sell them on to him in Biyassa Trenta, and he gave him his phone so the customer could contact him. Toba put the two grams in his mouth but as soon as he got to the garden, he saw the police waiting for him. It turns out that the customer had been caught with the two grams and the police had given him a choice of being arrested or calling Ashraf and asking for more. Naturally, he preferred they arrest Ashraf red-handed. Ashraf called himself Jimmie, so they caught Toba and said, Are you Jimmie? and he said, I'm not Jimmie. So they dialed Jimmie off the guy's phone and it rang in his pocket, and they took him into custody and he was tried and sentenced to eight months.

I used to sell at the Biyassa Trenta and Balats 42, which were both dangerous. The police could raid the place at any time and catch you red-handed. I kept looking for a safe place till I found a bar in Porta Romana that was so good for selling drugs without worries you might have thought it had been custom-made—high up and like a balcony looking over a garden, with two large sets of steps, so that when you were there you could see who was coming up them. Bang in front of it was an old fountain overgrown with reeds, so you could sit there with the drugs in your hand and if the police came just throw the stuff into the fountain and sit there like a regular person. Plus, before I discovered it, it had had no connection to drugs.

It was open every day, but Wednesday was party night and it would fill up completely with kids drinking and dancing till morning. I'd bring half a kilo of hashish, cut it up right there in the middle of them, and sell, so that in the end it came to be known as my bar. One night Hazem and I drank there and went home stinking drunk. I had some whiskey I was drinking straight from the bottle on the street, and as we crossed Biyassa Trenta a Tunisian kid stopped us and asked, Could you give me a drink, bro? I told him, No. He disgusted me because he went with guys in their cars in the garden. He said, Why are you fucking around, Egyptian? I said, *I'm* the one that fucks around, you son of a bitch? and threw the bottle down, pulled out my knife, set on him, and, *zip zap!*, cut his face open. He ran off covered in blood. That day I was wearing the Inter Milan T-shirt and, with the mustache and the bald head, I really stood out. The kid stopped a long way away at the end of the garden and called the police and I sat down where I was, too drunk to move, while Hazem kept telling me, Come on! The police are going to come! Come on! They'll arrest us! He was pulling at me, come on, come on, but nothing doing. It was hardly one street from where we were to the House of Abundance. You go out of the garden, cross a paved street, and go into the house. But I'd made up my mind I wasn't going to move till I saw what the son of a bitch Tunisian kid was going to do, so when Hazem saw he couldn't do anything with me, he left. Suddenly I saw a police car coming, so I got up and ran toward the station wall. I was going to jump over and my fingers had just got a grip, when somebody hit me on the head with the butt of his pistol so hard it left a bald patch that's there to this day. I fainted and fell, and they lifted me—*hupp!*—and put me into the car. When I came to, I found myself in a room alone on a bed at the police station and couldn't remember a thing.

Next morning, they took me to court and I found myself landed with a case of armed robbery. The Tunisian said I'd held him up, slashed him with a switchblade, and taken two hundred euros, a watch and a phone. They appointed me a lawyer called Maria Bianca—Fair Mariam—and I was remanded in custody for two months pending trial. They moved me to Reception, San Fakturya prison—search, strip, photo, fingerprints—gave me a blanket, cup, and eating utensils, and put me in a cell with four Moroccans and one Egyptian, plus a television and receiver. There I spent two months. All night long it was cards, dominoes, chess, and sex movies. Every morning you change the sheet. Every week you wash your clothes. And from one to five was exercise, in a very large garden surrounded by a high wall with guards on it coming and going with automatic weapons.

After two months, they brought me in front of the court and I made up a story. I told them, I live in Balats 42 and work in construction. The Tunisian is a drug dealer and I met him in Loreto about five months ago and we became friends. One day, as I was going into Balats 42, I met a bunch of Egyptians who were holding him, threatening him with knives, and swearing they were going to kill him because he'd taken drugs from them worth five hundred euros and hadn't paid them back. When he saw me, he pleaded with me to help him. He said, Save me! Please! God have mercy on your parents! So I got him out of their clutches and paid the five hundred euros. Later, I asked him for the money more than once but nothing doing. The last time, the day of the fight, he told me, Fuck off! I don't owe you anything. I got angry and hit him and the police came and arrested me. Then I asked that they let me confront him, face to face, so sentencing was postponed for three months pending the confrontation and I went back to San Fakturya.

At the prison, they give you drops and pills so you sleep and don't make problems. I became addicted to the pills—they're a strong tranquilizer that gets you high—and every time I ran out, I'd go crazy and scream and fight the guards and curse them, so they'd give me more. I sold the drops and got high on the pills.

The three months passed. The Tunisian never came for the confrontation, and the court established that he was a drug dealer and on the run from an eight-month sentence. The trial was postponed for three more months, and I made a fuss in court and cursed out the guards and even the judge. In the prison, I started making new problems every day. One time I'd beat up a Moroccan, another I'd throw the meal tray in the guard's face, and lots of times I refused to go back into my cell after exercise. Neither the pills nor the drops did any good, and I became famous in the prison—el-Baffo did this, el-Baffo did that. Finally my court session came, on 27 Ramadan, the

Night of Power. I did my ablutions and made two extra prostrations and I prayed and said, "Save me, O Lord! You know I didn't commit a robbery!" They took me to the court. For the big cases, where the sentence is five years or more, they don't put you in the dock or take you into a courtroom to begin with. It's just a small office with a judge. I, of course, was armed robbery, so they took me and the lawyer to an office. We waited out in front for a while and then they took us in. The lawyer and I sat down with the interpreter between us. I told the judge I was innocent: Put me in the same room with the Tunisian! He said, Wait outside, so I left the room and sat there fuming and like, Dear God! Dear God! The lowest sentence in a case like mine is five years! And finally, after I'd almost died, the lawyer came out and told me, Innocent! I was walking on air! I hugged her, threw her in the air, held her up there like a trophy, went back to San Fakturya, got my stuff, and said goodbye to my friends. On my way out, the director of the prison had a word with me. She knew me because of all the problems. She was really butch, I mean butch-butch, with frizzy hair, taller than me and a hulk. She shook my hand and said, Make sure you don't come back! Then I left.

An Historic Misconception

THERE IS A FIRMLY HELD historic misconception that what unifies Egypt is the Nile Valley, when the true unifying factor is the desert, where Libya is. Of course, there's colonialism and there's obviously a lot to be made out of the Nile Valley, "the artery of life." It's been proven that Sudan is no use whatsoever in this regard, or even actively harmful, and the Sudanese are different from us, even in color and language, while the Libyans can be thought of as Egyptians—a group of tribes most of whom have extensions in Egypt. The first political party in Libya had integration into Egypt at the top of its agenda.

Despite this, Egypt has always been united with, or tried to unite with, Sudan. Egypt has followed geography—or not geography but just the Nile—when it would have made more sense to follow and unite with human beings. The Sudanese scowl at us and harbor a grudge or some weird combination of scorn and disgust or whatever other kind of subterranean feeling, and it's indelible. I'd even go so far as to say that there isn't a single Sudanese to be found in you, my dear Sudan, who doesn't scowl at Egypt, including even those who love her, the crème of her crème and her artists. But Libyans are the same kind of human beings, have the same language, the same griefs and preoccupations, as well as the same singers and songs and fatwas and sheikhs and fleeting moments. Libya is truly a piece of Egypt, at any level you care to choose. It is no coincidence that every political current that has touched

Libya in the modern age has reproduced, letter for letter, whatever Egypt has experienced, including its Leader, who was nothing but a Libyan copy, albeit a tatty one, of Egypt's.

The Totoh Thing

I WENT TO THE HOUSE of Abundance and the moment I entered they yelled, Muhyi Bu Golayyel! and hugged me, and everyone started throwing money at me and they took me to the lab and we snorted cocaine till I was high as a kite. I saw there were new people with them, some visiting, some living there. Out of these, I became friends with Ahmad Umara, from Rashid. I discovered that it wasn't the old House of Abundance any more. Ashraf Bu Naasa, who'd become *capo* in my place, was a smart operator. He could pull anything off and he'd made the House of Abundance into the center of the drug trade for the whole of Milan. Balats 42, Milan's old drug stronghold, was nothing beside it now. The drug kingpins were just clients like any others: they came and got their share from the House of Abundance. The first thing I saw when I went in was Ali Balaha, who used to supply us before I went to jail, opening a travel bag with thirteen kilos of heroin in it, and thousands were being counted out before your eyes. People were coming from Palermo, Naples, and even Rome itself to get goods from the House of Abundance, and everyone was working in drugs. Even Fathi Laaraj, who used to hang about waiting for gays in Biyassa Trenta, was working with heroin and had his own customers and a bike that he went around on day and night delivering. In addition to Fathi Laaraj, there were other new people who'd moved in and I didn't know. They'd also got two Romanian women and put them up in the basement under the

House of Abundance, which we later turned into a lab for cutting cocaine—Umm Toba, who worked as a beggar, and her sister, who worked as a prostitute. Every morning they'd set off for the Sisyo Centrale. The beggar begged and the prostitute got fucked two or three times and made herself around five or six hundred euros and they'd come home at the end of the day loaded up with good things, from chickens to beer and wine.

Ashraf was the *capo*, and Ashraf had told them about Muhyi Bu Golayyel who'd shown the Tunisians off the premises, thrown out the Romanians, and put together the House of Abundance, and how everyone who came there now did so because of him. I worked with them, got a new telephone line, recovered my old clients, plus Ashraf gave me a few of his. We got the cocaine from Helal el-Fayoumi and the heroin from Ali Balaha and the money flowed and every night was a party. I dealt and drank and played the slot machines, and I got to know a bunch of Romanians living in the train station. One of them, called Alberto, had four women working the street for him, and I'd get a five-liter wine jar and a stick of hashish and spend the night partying with them. I'd pick one of them out, take her into any of the rooms, do it, and give her something, or not. They'd gone there for that anyway—the men to smuggle and steal, the women to whore. I ran the neighborhood and everyone was afraid of el-Baffo Saddam the Egyptian, and when we ran out of money and didn't even have enough to eat, I went to them and shook Alberto down. We were friends, so he couldn't believe it and said, Saddam this! Saddam that! I told him, Zip it! and took two hundred euros from him, then went and got the rest and we took everything they had and slept with the women. After that, he took his women, left the neighborhood, and never came back.

Then, *bam!*, Ashraf was caught. They nabbed him with fifty grams of cocaine and he got a year. Next Karim was caught. Ahmad Umara and I were left to deal the drugs and Hazem, Muhammad el-Sughayyar, and Lutfi were with us but shook down gays. Muhammad el-Zaim came. He'd been sent to prison for theft with a six-month sentence. He stayed with us at the House of Abundance for two days and took an apartment in Balats 42 and worked with us. He took stuff from us on consignment and moved it inside the Balats. One day, he got into a fight with a bunch of the guys there and they beat him, so he stabbed one of them in the heart with his knife and the guy died, so el-Zaim ran away and disappeared. The police knew he was a relative of mine and raided us at the House of Abundance and took me and Ahmad Umara, held us for two days, then let us out. The next night, when I was sitting at a slot machine in a bar, Ahmad Umara called me and said, Come right now!

What's up, kid?

He said, I'm telling you, come! So I went and I found el-Zaim sitting in the same spot I'd been sitting when the owner of the house approached me the first time. He'd been cut on his face and hand. I picked him up straight away and lowered him down to the lab. The police came, and then came again, but they didn't get into the lab, because when you look into it through the opening we used to get down by, all you're aware of is the garbage and the terrible smell. El-Zaim stayed there five days, with the police watching me all the time, and news of it got out. Even in Egypt they knew that el-Zaim had killed someone. I had a friend from Tatoun who was living in Famagosta. He'd been adopted by a French lady doctor who had three clinics, one in Italy, one in France, and one in Switzerland, and he spent the whole month going round with her in her car. She promised him she'd smuggle el-Zaim to France. From there he went to Belgium and from there he got out to Egypt.

There was an officer we used to call el-Muslo because of all the muscles in his body. He was watching me and every day, on the off-chance, he'd ask me, Where's el-Zaim, Baffo? I'd tell him, In Egypt, but he wouldn't believe me and he'd say, No, you're hiding him. In the end, I got sick of it and I told him, Hold on! and I called el-Zaim in Egypt and spoke to him in Italian and said, El-Muslo's standing in front of me and he doesn't believe you're in Egypt. Then I turned on the speaker and gave him the phone. He said, *Ciao!* and el-Zaim said, How are you, Muslo, you son of a whore? He asked him, Is that el-Zaim? He said, Sure, I'm el-Zaim. If you're a man, come to Egypt and us Bedouins will slit your throat in the desert. He gave me back the phone and asked, Who got him over there? I told him, How should I know? Get off my back. But I could feel he wasn't going to let me off— was he going to let go of the el-Zaim thing when el-Zaim had to go to jail?— and I could see them watching me as I dealt to the clients. Then what Hazem, Lutfi, and Muhammad el-Sughayyar did brought it all to a head.

The three of them worked on shaking down gays. They'd send Muhammad el-Sughayyar to one of them and as soon as things got going, shake him down and clean him out. Muhammad was cute-looking and he did top and bottom. He'd given us to understand that he did top but one time we were shaking someone down and by accident we found Muhammad with his pants off lying underneath the guy. He disappeared for a while, then came to see me at the House of Abundance with his tail between his legs and said, I know you're going to throw me out. I told him, No, son. It's your ass and you can do what you like with it.

Anyway, the three of them made a plan to shake down someone Muhammad was sleeping with, at the guy's home in a very deluxe apartment building in Loreto. Muhammad went to him the way he usually did, did it, left his wallet on the bed they'd been lying on, and went to where the other two were waiting downstairs. After a little, he called the guy and told him, I forgot my wallet, so the guy opened the door to the building for him and he went in, along with Hazem and Lutfi. They went into the guy's place, and held him up but he refused to be held up. He was tough and brave, unlike most of those guys, and refused to go along with them. They kept hitting one another for a bit till one of them stabbed him in the side with a large pair of scissors and he fell. They stole his laptop and two pairs of shoes of the kind that go for seven hundred euros a pair, two watches, a cell phone, and two thousand euros, and then came back to the House of Abundance and buried the laptop in the garden. All of which I knew nothing about.

The next day, Hazem and Muhammad took the laptop and went and sold it on Carlo Farini, where they were caught: the moment the guy who was going to buy it opened it, the police fell on them, and who did it turn out the laptop belonged to? A judge. And not just any judge: this guy was the head of Milan's judiciary, and the laptop had on it the original copy of the case against Totoh, the head of the Italian Mafia, and the secret police were looking for it everywhere.

All of a sudden, when we were sitting smoking a couple of joints in the parlor at the House of Abundance, more than sixty men wearing black, with masks and little black submachine guns surrounded us, and it was like, Don't move, and they cocked their weapons. Then a guy came in wearing a suit and necktie and said to me, Listen, Baffo. We're not police and we're not interested in the drugs that are sitting there in front of you. We want Lutfi. At that moment, Lutfi was staying right next to us on the second floor of the tower that's between the House of Abundance and the company. The stairway to it was broken and we used to get up there by a knotted rope and you pulled the rope up after you.

They took us away with them, and I rode with the tie guy in a private car, another car with four men in it behind us, and the sixty masked men disappeared. We went to a chic villa in a classy neighborhood, where everyone was wearing civilian clothes, and he sat down at a desk and told me the story. He told me that the judge's stab wound had reached the pericardium and that he was in hospital, between life and death—and if you want to live in Italy, or even just live, you'll have to cooperate and hand Lutfi over to us. The car you came in is going to take you back to the house. I swore on my mother's life that I didn't know anything and that I'd hand him over the moment I saw him, and then I went back and found Lutfi sitting with the boys in the parlor. I told him, You son of two hundred dogs! You killed some big-shot Christian and got filmed going in and out. Get your stuff and leave Italy completely, but by the time he'd climbed up into the tower, the sixty masked men had fallen on us. They'd been hidden in the forest and noticed the light go on in the tower, so they went in and seized him, beat him, and two of them picked him up by his arms and legs, swung him, and threw him from the second floor. He landed with a whump, said *Ahhhh!* and they told him, No. Don't die now! You're going to go through hell. You know who you stabbed, you filthy Egyptian? Then they took him away, but as they were going out, the tie guy looked at me and said, Be good, Baffo!

The Blue Corolla

In Sabha, I stayed with the son of my maternal aunt Nasaha. He was the type who loves fixing things, his own and other people's, without being asked and without any kind of skill. In fact, he usually makes a mess of what he's trying to fix and leaves it in twenty pieces. In Libya, he had a notion to work as a panel beater and body painter reasoning that they were a close match for his skills when it came to taking things apart and putting them together again. When I went to visit him at the workshop, he was working as an assistant panel beater and its main painter. The workshop was rented out by the highly skilled master craftsman Hadi the Tunisian. There was a restaurant at the workshop, where I worked—a small restaurant whose customers were some of the skilled workers from the industrial quarter. It was only large enough for one worker to cook, serve, and clean. I, as usual, got enthusiastic and focused on it with the same dumb intensity with which I always focus on things, and projects, and even people, only to discover—or not discover, it's just that my enthusiasm cools—that I had been deceived, and get sad.

When describing his own experience, my friend and closest soul-mate says of himself that it's like he's digging holes in the Mediterranean: he digs a deep hole and abandons it, and not just abandons it, he forgets about it and starts over with a new hole. Sisyphus, I swear, is our model: Sisyphus goes up, we go down, and I've taken over the hole from him.

The restaurant grew to be the largest and most crowded in the industrial quarter. I cooked simple things: omelet for breakfast and potatoes with meat for lunch, but with lots of extras and innovative ways of doing them. I felt that most of my customers had never seen food like mine anywhere, and they fell on it "as though from a great height." But the fact is what attracted them most was the cheap prices. We were, incontestably, the cheapest restaurant in Sabha. Hadi provided it with everything it needed and he paid me, and me alone among all the workers in the shop, in dollars. One day, my cousin had a fight with Hadi, or Eweidat, I can't remember, and left the workshop, so it became my obligation, from the tribal, or kinship, perspective to leave the restaurant and the workshop, because his mother was my aunt. When I was slow in making up my mind about the matter, he sent me a message to the effect that it was "shameful for you to stay with the workshop after your cousin has left it." Eweidat, the owner of the workshop, who was always quarrelling with me "patriotically," if I may put it that way, came to me and said, "You came to Libya to work and go back to your family, not play games in the street with your cousin." But I left along with my cousin and we moved to another workshop in the same industrial quarter, which turned out to be a meeting place for the worst sort of criminals in all of Sabha, and perhaps all of Libya.

One day, some enemies of theirs stormed the workshop at night, dead drunk, the goal of the attack not being the usual plunder or robbery but to teach them a lesson, meaning to wipe the floor with everyone there and beat them to the point of death. My brilliant cousin was alone in the workshop. (I have two aunts on my mother's side, one smart and wicked, the other proud and good-natured. The eldest of the three sisters is my naive—I'm too embarrassed to say retarded, which is what she says her wicked, successful, smart sister used to call her—mother. My smart aunt's son wasn't smart, and even my smart aunt got annoyed by his stupidity, lack of resourceful-ness, and failure in life.)

So, he got up, bewildered by the ruckus they were making in the cars, never intending to resist them or prevent them from stealing. They, though, were drunk and thought that all his bewilderment and shouting and barging about in the midst of them meant resistance, and they wiped the floor with him. It's also said that he did nothing out of the ordinary but they thought because they were so drunk that he was putting up a fight, so they beat him almost to death.

Anyway, my cousin decided he was going to work there as a panel beater and proper body painter and I was going to be his assistant. We did three cars. By Libyan standards, his work was acceptable or, at least, didn't rise, or maybe one should say fall, to a level that would attract attention to the fact that he was new to the profession. It made it easier for him that his customers were new to the world of automobiles, most of them having just shifted from camelback to car-back and hav-ing no idea of the difference between vehicle oil and cooking oil. This was what enticed and allured my cousin and led him into error. He decided he'd play around with the materials and he swapped expensive auto paint for cheap wood paint, with a little help from that celebrated Egyptian low cunning that says, "Anyway, it's all paint and they won't notice the dif-ference." His first experiment in his plan to economize on materials was a Toyota Corolla, just when Japan's first Corol-las came out and moved the history of automobile-making materially and immaterially—form, engine, comfort, every-thing. Its owner was a young Libyan wearing a turban—not the turban of a sheikh but that of a young man "with a good conceit of himself," as they say.

We worked on the Corolla for a week—panel work, sand-ing, and polishing, myself under his command, with bucket and towel. He sprayed the shiny metallic-blue Corolla with shiny green wood paint. I don't know why green when he could have bought blue for the same price. The owner descended from a Toyota Landcruiser with an automatic rifle parked on its seat. He went up to the Corolla and drew his long fingernail over the hood, making a trench in the wood paint, and said, in real panic and with appalling menace, "Wood paint too, you piss pants! I was going to kill you just for the green!" and he retreated to the Landcruiser and was like "I am now going to kill you, you thieves," and he pulled the automatic from the Toyota and cocked it. The only solution was for me to kiss his head. And, as I said, one may fear a thug to the point of terror but not be afraid of a weapon. Many a time a gun has been put to my head and I haven't felt any fear, just smiled a dumb smile. So I leaned forward over his head till the gun was rubbing against my chest and said to him, with true submission and infinite calm, "I beseech you, by the Prophet, we'll do it over!"

He said, "Fine, fine," and retreated. "I'll come back in a week."

So we brought in body-painting specialists at our own expense and a week later handed the car over to him as a shiny metallic-blue Toyota Corolla.

France

THE WAY I SAW IT, I was going to get picked up whatever happened. The police would arrest me—el-Zaim had run away to Egypt, Hazem, Lutfi, and Muhammad el-Sughayyar had each got eleven and a half years, and there was only me and Ahmad Umara left. So I gave him the SIM card with all the clients' names and went to see my friend who'd got el-Zaim into France and went off to France with him and his mother in their car with the smoked glass, him and his mother in front, me in the back. I had about three thousand euros with me, and I put up with one of us from the village who was staying in Paris, and he found me lodgings in the Qat'schuman neighborhood along with the Africans and the Arabs. The third day, I was walking in the street watching the world when I came across a Tunisian loading a fridge into a van. I helped him and we introduced ourselves and he asked me, Are you working? I said, No, I've just arrived and don't have a job. He said, Would you like to work with me? I said, That would be great. What work do you do? He said, Stucco. We agreed he'd call me in the morning and I forgot about the whole thing, thinking he'd be like the guys in Italy. A thousand guys must have told me, I'll give you work, and didn't. I didn't even take down his number but finished my stroll and went home and spent the evening watching porn movies and then slept. But at six in the morning my phone began to ring and ring, and I woke and there he was, asking me, What's the matter? Don't you want to work? I said, No, I do, I do. He said, Okay, come. I'm waiting in Qat'schuman now, so I got dressed and went down and I found the work was very easy. Ready-made plaster casts that we mounted on ceilings and walls. I put in ten months of work with him and didn't take a single day off.

I visited the Eiffel Tower and Pigalle Street, the one that Sheikh Kishk said was "a subdivision of Hell." It turned out to be a street where men and women were displayed in shop windows with the utmost explicitness, as well, of course, as everything that goes with that, like medications, creams, foods, clothes, and all the rest of it. I took to strolling round the gardens till I came across a bunch of Algerians selling hashish. I bought some from them—here's looking at you, Europe!— and we became friends. I'd visit with them and they'd visit with me and every Sunday night we'd go out to bars and discotheques. Things started looking up for me and I sent money to my family for the first and last time. I got to know the sister of the Tunisian guy I was working with. She was married to an Algerian lout who mounted her from behind. Why? So he could hit her on the head with his shoe! We went for walks together in the gardens and she took me to the movies, which was the first and last movie house I went into in Europe. She used to come and see me in the apartment every Sunday and we'd cook and spend the day together.

One day, Hatem Bu el-Mazzaz came to see me. He was on the run from Italy and had spent six months looking for work without finding any. He was starving and he said, I want to go back to Italy but I don't have the money for the ticket. I'd just been paid, so I took him to the train station but instead of asking the ticket lady for one ticket, I asked for two, and by the time I realized my mistake, she'd issued them and somehow, I don't know how, at that moment I decided to go back to Italy. All I had was the clothes on my back and a ball of hashish weighing about a quarter of a *qirsh*, so I picked up Hatem's bag and we stood in line to get on the train. A small black and white dog with frizzy hair came up to me and started sniffing at the pocket where the hashish was. I pretended to play with him and kept pushing him away but it made no difference, and I felt someone tap me on the shoulder from behind. I turned and he showed me a police ID and said, The bag, please, and he bent down, opened it, and started going through it, so I shoved my hand into my pocket, took out the piece of hashish and put it into my mouth while the dog kept looking at me, his eyes sending out sparks, or that's what it felt like. The man went through the bag, said, Thank you, and moved away, but the dog kept looking at me and refusing to budge, so the man came back to me, took a piece of cotton wool out of his pocket, waved it four times at the dog's nose and the dog shook its head and went off behind the man, still looking at me.

We got on the train and the moment we'd sat down I said to Hatem, I don't know why, I'm going to Italy to go to prison, and at the French-Italian border, the Italian police got on and took us off and handed us over to the French police, but not to put us in jail. On the contrary, the French asked us, Do you want to go to Italy or stay in France? We said Italy, so they put us on the next train.

Pharaoh Boy

So I WENT BACK TO Milan. First of all, I went to Balats 42, Tareq Bu el-Dahab's place. He was an Egyptian in his fifties from the Fayoum and had come to Italy around thirty years ago. He'd been a big contractor, and maybe he put up a big apartment building and it fell down or something else happened that shafted him, who knows? So he let his beard grow and began behaving like a dervish and sat drinking day and night in front of the Castello pretending to the Italians he was mad. I'd gotten to know him there and had taken him with me to the House of Abundance and told everyone he was a sheikh of the Baraasi Bedouin, though he wasn't a Baraasi or even a Bedouin.

I stayed with him for two days, then went to the House of Abundance, where the only person I found was Karim. He was around thirty and from el-Mansoura. He spoke Italian better than he did Arabic because he'd come when he was fifteen and they'd given him residency because he was a minor. With the residency he was able to work as a driver at a big company. Once he'd got drunk and had a fight with the police and hit an officer on the head with a bottle, so they took his residency and his driver's license away from him and left him on the street, till I found him in the van and put him to work as a cook in the House of Abundance, and he got a cut just like the rest of us. When I went to jail the first time, Ashraf Bu Naasa put him to work on the drugs. With his language and his quick wits, he did well and got lots of customers, working like hell out of two numbers—his own, and the one I'd left for Ahmad Umara—and was pulling in not less than five thousand euros a day. Now he gave me back my SIM card and we worked together, paying for the goods together and splitting the profit.

We got the goods from the Albanians, and we did well. We kept the storeroom at the House of Abundance for wholesale and took two apartments in one building in Famagosta, one on the first floor for retail and distribution, one on the third floor for us. We began taking three-carton consignments from the Albanians, each carton twenty-five kilos of heroin, and that was in addition to the cocaine, and we worked both. We eased up on the one- and two-gram stuff and began distributing by the kilo, and we'd clear five thousand euros a day, not counting the food and drink, with the slot machines as a variable. At the end of the week, we'd get together and I'd fetch my Italian girlfriend Toka and we'd go in our car to a large casino or any *distatika* we fancied. Usually, we'd go to a night-club with a large casino on the road to Bergamo, which goes to France. We'd drink, dance, and spend whatever we had with us on playing roulette and we'd get back in the morning dead drunk and without a cent. And then we'd return to the attack. That was how we lived our lives. We saw the beauty and the pleasure of life and we spent our nights with the youth of Italy, America, Spain, and the whole world.

Then suddenly we quarreled. We were at the bar and I was drunk. He told me, Go get ten grams from the lab, and I told him, No, I'm going to sleep, you go, and I went out, leaving him at the bar. He got mad and broke the bottle he was holding and muttered something. When I got to the house, I thought about it and decided he was right. In the end, the work was for us both, so I went and got the ten grams from the lab and I'd barely had time to get out the stuff and start breaking it up before a friend of mine, who'd been at the bar when we quarreled, rushed in and said, Pick it up! Pick it up! Karim informed on you! I picked up all the stuff, stashed it away, left the House of Abundance, jumped over the wall and walked in the direction of the railroad. I had just come out through the gap that goes down to the road, when I found the police in front of me and it was like, Hold it right there! Where are you coming from? I told them I'd got taken short and gone out to relieve myself. They asked me, Do you know the owner of this phone number? I looked and saw it was my number, so I told them, No, I don't even have a phone to begin with. They called it and it rang in the house so they left me.

I went to the house and slept normally, as though the police had never stopped me. In the morning, I went up to Karim in the bar. He had half a kilo of heroin with him. He gave me ten grams and told me, There's a customer coming. Sell them on them to him and catch up with me at the lab. I'll have broken up the half-kilo and we can start moving the customers.

He'd barely left before the customer arrived so I sold the stuff to him and rushed after him. I went down into the lab and found him sitting there, and he still hadn't gotten the half-kilo out. I screamed at him, Stand up, you son of a whore! He asked me, What's up, Bu Golayyel? Have you gone crazy? I said, You want to send me to jail, you son of a bitch? You want to send me to jail, you son of a whore? and I pulled out my knife and was like, Hand over everything you've got on you, let's go, and I took five thousand euros and the half-kilo and his phone off him and told him, Get out of here, and if I see your face around here again, I'll cut your throat.

I worked for a time on my own. Then Ahmad Umara came and I put him to work with me. Exactly twenty days later, me and him and Bu el-Dahab were spending the evening in a bar opposite Balats 42 (Via Bligny, which connects Porta Romana and Porta Genova) and we got dead drunk. Me and Umara left to snort some cocaine to sober us up. Bu el-Dahab came outside with us and stood in front of the bar, and we'd barely left him and not even gone ten meters when we heard him yell, Bu Go*laaay*el! I turned round and saw a Tunisian lift him up, slam him down onto the ground, and kneel on his chest. We came back, grabbed the Tunisian, pummeled the daylights out of him, and Bu el-Dahab slashed him with a knife as he ran off. As he was running, I noticed he'd dropped a cell phone, which slid under a car, and I told Ahmad Umara to get it. He said, It's an old Sony Erikson and wouldn't fetch ten euros. I told him, Give it here. He gave it to me and I stuffed it in my pocket, and as we were walking down the side of Giardino Heweidi I saw a police car coming out from it. It was two-thirty and like, Good evening, good evening, where are you going? We said, Home. Where do you live? We said, Balats No. 8. Very well, would you mind showing us what you have on you? I brought out everything I had on me, including the phone belonging to the Tunisian, and the moment he saw it he spoke on his walkie-talkie and said, *Trovato*, meaning, Found it, and suddenly there was a car on this side and a car on that, and they took us to the station. The Tunisian had made a report that we'd committed armed robbery and taken the phone from him plus two thousand euros and a gold chain, and the next day they moved us to San Fakturya.

As soon as I entered, it was like, Oh-oh! Not you again, Diyab! and they put us in a *cella* with two Egyptians and two Moroccans. After two or three days we got into a quarrel with one of the Moroccans and closed the door to the cell and beat him to within an inch of his life. They took him to the hospital and the whole jail knew. A little later, they called for anyone who wanted to go to the *falmaria*, meaning the lady doctor, but they called us to go with them even though we weren't sick and hadn't asked to go to the *falmaria*. I told Ahmad, They're setting us up for something, for sure, and I grabbed a couple of razor blades and tucked them under my tongue. They took the prisoners in to the doctor and took us—me and Ahmad Umara— to the Rotunda, the old prison, which has a large ring in the middle with the office of the prison's *bregadeer* at the side plus five doors, each of which opens onto a seven-story wing, and which has a large dome in the form of a five-pointed star with a huge cross mounted above it. As soon as we reached the middle of the ring, fifteen men, each twice my size, came out through the doors. They were wearing all black and I could see only their eyes. Gloves, black masks, and leather truncheons. The doors closed. *Tramp tramp tramp* and the area turned into one huge cell. The *bregadeer* came out in front of his office and said to me, Now I'm going to see what that pharaonic stuff they keep talking about is really made of. You think you're *pharaonic* and can beat up the Moroccan, but we don't allow beating, and if you beat you get beaten. I told him, *Adesso guardi* the *pharaonic*—now you'll see what pharaonic is—and I pulled off the T-shirt I had on and flipped it round my hand and arm and was left wearing just my boxers. Then *tirikk!* I pulled out the two razors and immediately *zippp!* from my shoulder to my left side with one of the razors and *zippp!* with the other from my shoulder to my right side, and I was covered in blood. The director shouted, Enough! Enough, you madman! and I said, You want to see more Baffo the Pharaoh? and *zippp!* with the razor across my head. He said, Enough enough enough! and he turned to the fifteen masked oxen and yelled at them, Get out of here! I had gotten blood all over the ring and they had to go on begging me for a good while before I threw down the razors and went to the doctor, who sewed me up. They took me and put me in solitary but I wouldn't have it and started pulling the bandages off my chest and head and breaking the stitches. They said, Okay, okay, we'll do whatever you want, and they took me back to the doctor, who sewed me up again, and then to the director, who said, the moment I went into her office, Not you again, Diyab! I told her, I want to go back to my old place, so she sent me back there. They'd put Ahmad Umara in solitary, so after a little I asked the director to send him back and she did.

The same back-and-forth I'd set up the first time I was in jail I did again now with Ahmad Umara. We agreed that we didn't know one another, that I'd come to the bar and found him sitting with his Albanian girlfriend, and that I'd quarreled with the Tunisian and we'd begun fighting because of money he owed me that I'd asked him for more than once and that he hadn't paid: So your girlfriend tells you, That's how Arabs are, so you got in between us and got his phone off him for me, with his agreement, as a guarantee for my money. Ask the Albanian girl! She'll tell you that's what happened. Then the judge asked me, And what about the cut on his face? And we were caught out. We didn't know Bu el-Dahab had slashed the Tunisian with a razor. The court was adjourned for three months and we went back to San Fakturya.

We heard that Karim was working hell-for-leather and that he'd informed on Ashraf Bu Naasa and got him put in jail again, so I put my head through the cell window and shouted at the top of my voice, Kar*iiiiim*! because there's a custom, or a belief, in prison that if you call out to someone when you're there they'll come to you, not as a visitor but as an inmate, and exactly one month after I called to Karim I was lying down when the cell door opened and, *bam!*, it closed again, and I sat up and found Karim, shaking like a leaf. I said, Welcome! He told me, I swear I didn't inform on you! He got eight months.

One day, an inmate who had a job in the prison told me that a Palestinian called Basem Khalil down on the first floor was asking after me. I knew it must be Fathi Laaraj. He'd identified himself to the authorities as Palestinian and always insisted that he was. So I went down and sat with him for a while and then I went to the director and pleaded with her till she agreed to move him into our cell.

The date of the hearing came and I insisted we hadn't beaten up the Tunisian and that I didn't know Ahmad Umara. I told the judge, The Tunisian's a drug dealer and he slashed himself to implicate us. She asked me, What proof do you have? I said, Let me meet him face to face and I'll prove to you that he owes me money and I wasn't the one who hit him—hoping that he'd be on the run, like the one before him, and my case was adjourned for three months and the Tunisian never turned up and I was declared innocent.

We got out and worked together, with the Albanians, and after four months Ahmad Umara was arrested. Karim had got out two months before and apologized to me again and said he'd been drunk and didn't know what he was doing. We worked together but I kept my eye on him. We worked together for three years, getting our stuff from two Albanians and passing it on to the Moroccans, Tunisians, and Egyptians all around Milan, and Moroccans started coming to us from Naples and Palermo wanting five cartons at a time. When we asked the Albanians to increase our quota, they took us to see the big-money guys in a bar outside Milan that belonged to a Moroccan. In front we saw four cars—one Ferrari, one BMx6, and two Hummers. As soon as the Albanians saw them, they said, The guys are here, and we went in. I took a good look at the people who were sitting there. They were in a corner that was curtained off and they had guards, who were sitting have a good time with a heap of Moroccan women. We waited outside and the Albanians went in and were gone for a quarter-hour and then they came out and got us. We went in and found they were old guys, over sixty, and scary to look at. So you're the Egyptians? Yes. And which of you is Saddam the Egyptian? I said, Me. Where from? I said, Asyut, Christian. He said, How much do you want? I said, Twenty-five cartons. Will you be able to pay? I said, Sure, and if you want more I can give it to you but after we move them. He said, Fine. The way he was talking to me I felt he was a bit stuck up and putting on the dog so I told him, Listen, I'm not afraid of anybody. I don't owe you anything and you don't owe me anything and I'm a man just like you. So when you speak to me, speak with respect. You've got money and you've made it, and I'm sure that by my own efforts I'll get to where you are and more too. So back off a bit. He said, Bravo! You've got a lot of confidence and you'll make it. Then he said, You guys wait for me outside. Give me half an hour and then come back. And in half an hour a truck pulled up in front of the bar with twenty-five cartons in it. We took them and put them upstairs in the apartment and in less than a month they were sold and we paid them 3.7 million euros and took twenty-five more cartons. He said, Take fifty. I told him, No. We blew the money on nights out, gambling and roulette, spending whatever we made. One time Karim would go get a carton, one time I would, till one day we went into the storeroom and found only two cartons and all we had was 200,000 euros. We were shocked. This could only mean death. The Albanians don't mess around with stuff like that. I'd handed a Moroccan to them once with my own hands and they'd killed him. There was nothing to do but run. I told Karim I was going to France to get money from my relatives there. Then I made a dash for Egypt.

Translator's Acknowledgments

THE TRANSLATOR THANKS CARMINE CARTOLANO and Patricia Newbery for their help with Italian and French place names.

Glossary

1st of September Revolution	a military coup carried out on this date in 1969 by the Free Officers' Movement headed by Colonel Muammar el-Gaddafi that toppled the Libyan monarchy.
A Dog With No Tail	a novel by Hamdi Abu Golayyel, translated by Robin Moger. AUCP, 2010; winner of the 2008 Naguib Mahfouz Award.
Abd el-Halim Hafez	a highly popular Egyptian singer (1929–77).
Abd el-Hamid	i.e., Abd el-Hamid Bu Erfan.
alam	a philosophical introduction to a *qasida* or Bedouin sung poem.
Alamein, El	a town on Egypt's northwest coast.
Amr ibn el-As	Muslim general who conquered Egypt (642).
el-Amriya	an industrial district west of Alexandria.
Aouzou	a village and oasis in the Aouzou Strip, claimed to be rich in uranium, in the extreme north of Chad; Aouzou was captured by Libyan forces in 1973 and returned to Chadian sovereignty in 1994.

Asyut   a city in Upper Egypt with a large
                        Christian population.

el-Ataba   the district surrounding a large square
                        of the same name in downtown Cairo
                        with many open-air stalls selling sec-
                        ondhand clothes.

Awad Bu Abd   see Awad el-Malki.
el-Gader el-Malki

Awad Bu Gaddoura   see Awad el-Malki.

Awad el-Malki   i.e., Awad Bu Abd el-Gader (or Bu
                        Gaddoura) el-Malki, a renowned
                        Bedouin singer.

el-Azhar   a millennial mosque and university in
                        Cairo.

el-Aziziya   a compound in Tripoli containing
                        Muammar el-Gaddafi's residence,
                        barracks, etc.; also known as Bab
                        el-Aziziya.

Azmi   a member of the Azayim Bedouin
                        tribe of the Western Desert.

Balats 42   i.e., Palazzo 42.

Bani Suleim   a Bedouin tribe, originally from the
                        Arabian Peninsula, that accompanied
                        the Banu Helal on the latter's west-
                        ward migration from Egypt into Libya,
                        where many still live, and further west.

Banu Helal   a Bedouin tribe, originally from the
                        Arabian Peninsula, that was forced
                        westward out of Egypt in the eleventh
                        century.

Banu Umayya   dynasty of caliphs founded by Mar-
                        wan ibn Abu Sufyan in 661 and
                        replaced by the Abbasids in 750;
                        sometimes taken in Arab lore as
                        emblematic of tyranny.

Parco La Fatitsi	an unidentified location in Milan (Parco degli Basiliche?).
Beheira	an area of northwestern Egypt.
el-Beida	a town on Libya's eastern coast, west of Tobruk and east of Benghazi.
Benghazi	a city on the coast of eastern Libya.
Biyassa Trenta	i.e., Piazza 30.
bregadeer	i.e., *brigadiere* (Italian: title applied loosely to police or army officers of any rank).
Bu Erfan	Abd el-Hamid Bu Erfan, an Egyptian officer at a police post on the Libyan border, named in "The Smuggler's Ballad."
Bu Gargour	a Libyan Bedouin famed for his skills as a master of ceremonies at weddings, a role that includes singing and reciting poetry.
bunta	i.e., *ponte* (Italian: "bridge").
the Castello	i.e., the Sforza Castle, near the Parco Sempione in Milan.
Chosroes	name of several of the Sassanian kings of Iran, who were often taken in Arab lore as emblematic of tyranny.
the Citadel	a fortress overlooking Cairo built by Saladin, seat of Egypt's government from its construction during the thirteenth century until the second half of the nineteenth century.
the Citadel of Qaitbey	a fifteenth-century fortress on the coast at Alexandria.
Cors el-Lodi	i.e., Corso Lodi, a major street running southeast from Porta Romana in central Milan.
the Cowboy	i.e., US President Ronald Reagan.

Danyal	a village in southern Fayoum.
distatika	i.e., "discotheque" (It.: *discoteca*).
the Domo	i.e., the Duomo, the cathedral church of Milan.
Ebshaway	a town in the Fayoum.
el-Edwa	a town near Minya in Upper Egypt.
effendi	a term formerly used to describe middle-class Egyptian men who wore European clothes.
emir	a Mameluke military commander.
Etsa	a town and district in southern Fayoum.
faddan	a square measure, slightly larger than an acre (4200.833 m^3).
falmaria	i.e., "pharmacy" (It.: *farmacia*).
Famagosta	the area around Viale Famagosta, southwest of the historic center of Milan.
Fatimid	pertaining to the Fatimid dynasty, which ruled Egypt from 909 to 1171.
Fayoum, the	a large oasis, holding numerous towns and villages, on the western side of the Nile valley, whose northern edge lies about one hundred kilometers southwest of Cairo.
fum . . . fumo	Italian: *fumo*, "smokes, cigarettes."
furbo	Italian: "smart, cunning."
el-Gaddafi	the family name of Muammar el-Gaddafi; from *gaddaf*, meaning "blood-spattering."
galabiya	Egyptian man's traditional closed robe.
Gamal Abd el-Nasser	leader of the coup that overthrew the Egyptian monarchy in 1952 and president of the country from 1954 to 1970.

Gamal Hamdan	eminent Egyptian geographer (1928–93).
el-Gharg	a hamlet in the southern Fayoum, west of Danyal.
ghinnawa	a short sung poem usually about love.
Giza	the area, now largely urbanized, on the west bank of the Nile opposite Cairo.
gol el-ajwad	Bedouin poetry recited without accompaniment; literally, "the speech of noble men."
the Good Book	the Qur'an.
the Great Betrayal	term used to characterize Egypt's 1973 signing of a peace treaty with Israel by its opponents.
the Great Manmade River	a system of underground pipelines and reservoirs that brings water from a fossil aquifer in southern Libya to the country's towns and cities; the project, which consists of five phases, was initiated in 1991 and is as yet incomplete.
The Green Book	a book by Muammar el-Gaddafi not dissimilar to Mao Tse-tung's "Little Red Book," in which the author sets out his political philosophy; first published in 1971, it grew in length with subsequent editions. All Libyans were expected to read it and it was widely drawn on by the regime for slogans.
Juhsi	name of Muammar el-Gaddafi's branch of the Gaddafi clan.
Hajj	title of a man who has made the Muslim pilgrimage to Mecca.

Hamad Basha el-Basel	leader of the Rimah Bedouin tribe of the Fayoum and supporter of Umar el-Mukhtar in his resistance to the Italian occupation of Libya (1871–1940).
Hasan el-Asmar	an Egyptian popular singer (1959– 2011), at the height of his fame in the 1970s and 1980s.
the Heavens the and Morning-star	phenomena invoked in the Qur'an (el-Tariq 86:1) in a chapter that stresses man's helplessness before his creator.
the House of Abundance	a villa near the old railroad station taken as a headquarters by the Phantom Raider and his associates.
Ibrahim el-Koni	a Libyan novelist of Tuareg background (b. 1948).
el-Jmeil	a city on the Libyan coast, close to the border with Tunisia.
King Idris el-Senousi	first and last king of independent Libya (r. 1951–69).
Kingi Maryout	an area in the Western Desert on the coast near Alexandria that has been developed in recent decades for tourism.
Lady A'isha	A'isha, the third and favorite of the wives of the Prophet Muhammad; the incident with Safwan ibn Muattal, a young Muslim warrior, ended with the exoneration of both.
Leader, the	see *Muammar el-Gaddafi*.
Loreto	i.e., Piazzale Loreto, a square in northeast Milan and the surrounding neighborhood.

Llosa	i.e., Mario Vargas Llosa, Peruvian novelist and intellectual (b. 1939).
el-Maamoura	a seaside district of the city of Alexandria.
Maghagha	a city in Upper Egypt's Minya governorate, on the west bank of the Nile.
majruda	a Bedouin long strophic poem usually addressed to a woman.
majruna	a wind instrument with a reed used in Bedouin music.
malzuma	a Bedouin verse form in which a poet writes two lines, then circulates them to other poets to complete.
Mameluke	a member of a military caste that in effect ruled Egypt during the late eighteenth century, despite the presence of an Ottoman governor.
el-Mansoura	a city in the northern Nile Delta.
Mashrigi	a member of a Bedouin tribe from eastern Libya.
Matrouh	a town on Egypt's western coast, close to the Libyan border; also called Mersa Matrouh.
el-Menoufiya	a governorate north of Cairo.
misr	a term that may mean both "any large city" or "Egypt."
Misrata	Libya's third-largest city, one hundred and eighty-seven kilometers east of Tripoli on the Mediterranean coast.
Muammar el-Gaddafi	ruler of Libya from 1969 to 2011; born c.1942.
Muhammad Ali Basha	ruler of Egypt, nominally as a subject of the Ottoman Empire, from 1805 to 1848 and founder of a dynasty that lasted until 1953.

Muhammad el-Seif-ert, Hajj	a Libyan Bedouin poet, intimate of former King Idris, and opponent of Muammar el-Gaddafi.
el-Muizz ibn Badis	a ruler of the Zirid dynasty (ruled 1016–62) of present-day Libya and Tunisia who rebelled against his Fatimid overlords in 1045.
Musaed	a Libyan village close to the Egyptian border.
Mustagab	Mohamed Mustagab, Egyptian novelist and short-story writer (1938–2006).
el-Mustansir Billah	a Fatimid dynasty ruler of Egypt (1036–94).
el-Mutanabbi	an Arab poet (d. 965) many of whose verses have become proverbial.
naviglio	any of several medieval canals that run through Lombardy and connect in Milan.
Nasr	literally, "Victory"; the trade name of many items produced in Egypt during its Arab Socialist period.
the Night of Power	a night during Ramadan (usually said to be the twenty-seventh) when it is believed that all prayers are answered.
Nubian	member of a people living historically in Nubia, the part of the Nile Valley between the first and sixth cataract of the Nile.
October 73 War, the	the war of that date between Egypt and Israel.
Umar el-Mukhtar	leader (b.1858–d.1931) from 1911 until his death of eastern Libyan resistance to Italian occupation.

Qat'schuman	i.e., Quatre Chemins, a métro stop and surrounding neighborhood on the northeast outskirts of Paris.
qirsh	a finger-shaped piece of hashish, so called because traditionally it was weighed against a piaster coin (*qirsh*).
el-Rabayea *or* el-Rubeiat	a Bedouin tribe based in Giza.
Ramadan	the ninth month of the Islamic calendar, during which Muslims fast from sunrise to sunset.
Rashid	a city on the eastern branch of the Nile close to its mouth.
the Rimah	an Egyptian Bedouin tribe based in the Fayoum.
el-Rubeiat	see *el-Rabayea*.
Rumhi	a member of the Rimah Bedouin tribe.
the Saad-Shin	literally, "[holders of] the Eastern Desert [card]" from the first letters of the Arabic words *el-Sahra' el-Sharqiya*, which have that meaning; i.e., Bedouin from other countries (especially Egypt) who were granted the right to work and other privileges by Libya during the rule of Muammar el-Gaddafi and sometimes recruited into his armed forces.
el-Sadat	Anwar el-Sadat, president of Egypt from 1970 to 1981.
Safwan ibn Muattal	See *Lady A'isha*.
el-Sarira	a hamlet near Danyal in the Fayoum.

Salafists	members of an Islamic movement that seeks to follow and impose beliefs and practices supposedly in accordance with those of the first three generations of Muslims, purged of all accretions.
Salloum	a town on Egypt's northwest coast, at the border with Libya.
San Fakturya	i.e., San Vittore, a prison in central Milan.
el-Senousi	See *King Idris el-Senousi*.
Sharm el-Sheikh	a resort town on Egypt's Red Sea coast.
el-Sharqiya	a governorate in northeast Egypt.
Sheikh Kishk	Abd el-Hamid Kishk (1933–96), an Islamist preacher.
shteiwa	**a Bedouin ring dance of clapping men with women in the middle.**
Sirte	a city on the Libyan coast about halfway between Tripoli and Benghazi; by some accounts, the birthplace of Muammar el-Gaddafi.
Sisyo	i.e., *Statione* (Italian: "station"), as in Sisyo Centrale: Milan's Central Station.
Sisyoni	= Sisyo
Suq el-Khamis	a daily market in Misrata, northwestern Libya; literally, the Thursday Market.
Tatanya	i.e., Catania, a port on Sicily's eastern coast.
Tatoun	a hamlet in the southern Fayoum, east of Danyal.

Third International Theory	a political, economic, and social creed based on direct democracy that was promulgated by Muammar el-Gaddafi in the early 1970s as the basis for the Great State of the Masses (also known as the Great Socialist People's Libyan Arab Jamahiriya).
Tobruk	a city on Libya's eastern coast, between Benghazi and the Egyptian border.
Tuareg	a Berber confederation found from southwestern Libya to southern Algeria, Niger, Mali and Burkina Faso.
Toubou	a people inhabiting northern Chad, southern Libya, northeastern Niger, and northwestern Sudan.
Umm el-Araneb	a village on the outskirts of Sabha, southern Libya.
Usama	Usama el-Denasuri (1960–2007), Egyptian poet and novelist, friend of the author.
Yaser, family of	a family of early converts to Islam in Mecca, who suffered greatly at the hands of the city's non-Muslim leaders and whom the Prophet Muhammad comforted with the words, "Patience, O Family of Yaser!"
Yasser Arafat	Palestinian leader (1929–2004), chairman of the Palestine Liberation Organization and president of the Palestine National Authority.
Zliten	a city on the Libyan coast, about one hundred and sixty kilometers east of Tripoli.

Zuwara	a city on Libya's Mediterranean coast, near the Algerian border.
Zuweila Gate	a large gate in medieval Cairo's southern wall.